MATT AND TO

ULTIMATE
FOOTBALL HEROES

GRIEZMANN
MBAPPE

FROM THE PLAYGROUND
TO THE PITCH

DINO

Published by Dino Books,
an imprint of Bonnier Books UK,
The Plaza,
535 Kings Road,
London SW10 0SZ

@dinobooks
@footieheroesbks
www.heroesfootball.com
www.bonnierbooks.co.uk

Griezmann first published 2019
Mbappe first published 2018
This collection published in 2020

Design and typesetting by www.envydesign.co.uk

ISBN: 978 1 78741 798 4

British Library Cataloguing-in-Publication Data:
A catalogue record for this book is available from the British Library.

Printed and bound in Great Britain by Clays Ltd, Elcograf S.p.A.
1 3 5 7 9 10 8 6 4 2

Matt Oldfield delivers sports writing workshops in schools,

and is the author of *Unbelievable Football* and *Johnny Ball:*

Accidental Football Genius. Tom Oldfield is a freelance sports

writer and the author of biographies on Cristiano Ronaldo,

Arsène Wenger and Rafael Nadal.

Cover illustration by Dan Leydon.
To learn more about Dan visit danleydon.com
To purchase his artwork visit etsy.com/shop/footynews
Or just follow him on Twitter @danleydon

GRIEZMANN

TABLE OF CONTENTS

CHAPTER 1

THE BIGGEST FINAL OF ALL

15 July 2018, Luzhniki Stadium, Moscow

One by one, the players walked along the quiet tunnel and out into an amazing spectacle of sound and colour. Yes, it was time for the 2018 World Cup final – France vs Croatia!

The France captain Hugo Lloris led the way, followed by defenders Raphaël Varane and Benjamin Pavard. It was a team full of superstars and their three biggest superstars were at the back of the line:

Kylian Mbappé – the 'next big thing' and the fastest footballer on the planet, Paul Pogba – a powerful midfielder who could play the perfect pass, and last but by no means least, their skilful Number

7, Antoine Griezmann.

Grizou! Grizou! Grizou!

Antoine was already a fans' favourite and a national hero, but if he could help France to win their second World Cup, he would become one of his country's true footballing legends. From Zinedine 'Zizou' Zidane in 1998 to 'Grizou' in 2018.

So far, everything was going according to plan. Antoine had led France all the way to the final, with three key goals and two key assists. When his team needed him most, he hadn't let them down. Whether he was scoring himself or setting up his teammates, Antoine's left foot was lethal!

One more win – that was all France now needed to pick up football's ultimate prize. Antoine was determined to bring joy to his country. He had lost big finals in the past – the 2016 Champions League with Atlético Madrid, Euro 2016 with France – but this was the biggest final of all: the World Cup final.

'And whatever it takes,' he told himself, 'I'm going to win it!'

As the national anthem played, Antoine sang the

words loudly and proudly. Although he had left
the country at the age of thirteen to move to Real
Sociedad in Spain, he still felt French. Mâcon was his
home and it always would be. He went back as often
as he could to visit his family and friends. They were
all cheering him on tonight, whether in the stadium
in Russia, or back home on TV.

The France fans were outnumbered by the
Croatians but as the match kicked off, they made as
much noise as possible.

Allez Les Bleus! Allez Les Bleus!

In the seventeenth minute, Raphaël passed to
Antoine, who spun quickly and... *FOUL! – FREE
KICK!*

As he got back to his feet, Antoine smiled to
himself. It was the perfect position for one of his
dangerous deliveries. He had set up Raphaël's goal in
the quarter-final and then Samuel Umtiti's goal in the
semi-final. Could he keep it up in the World
Cup final?

Antoine took a deep breath and waited for the
referee's whistle. Then he curled the ball into the

six-yard box and hoped for the best. Could anyone get a touch on it? Raphaël made a late run and leap to reach it but instead, it bounced off Mario Mandžukić's head and into the back of the net. *Own goal – 1–0 to France!*

'Yes, yes, YES!' Antoine roared as he skidded across the grass on his knees, just like he used to do as a kid. It was another key assist to add to his collection. They were on their way to World Cup glory...

But Croatia, like France, were a team who never gave up. Ten minutes later, the score was 1–1. Antoine would have to save the day with another set-piece. From his corner kick, Blaise Matuidi jumped up and missed the ball, but it struck Ivan Perišić on the arm.

'Handball!' the France players argued.

After checking with VAR, the referee said yes. *Penalty!*

Antoine placed the ball down carefully on the spot and took a few steps back. His penalty miss in the 2016 Champions League final was in the past now. France could rely on him; he hadn't missed one in ages.

But should Antoine aim for bottom left or bottom right, top corner, or straight down the middle with a cheeky Panenka chip? No – when the time came, Antoine kept things calm and simple, and sent the goalkeeper the wrong way.

Goooooooooooooooooooooaaaaaaaaaaaaaaaaalllllllllllll llllllllllllllll!!!!!!!!!!!!!!!!!!!!

An assist and now a goal – it was turning out to be Antoine's dream final. He celebrated by doing his 'Take the L' *Fortnite* dance, swinging his legs from side to side. His teammates were too cool to join in, but lots of France fans in the crowd did. 'Grizou' was their hero!

In this final in Moscow, the biggest final of all, Antoine was playing with so much confidence. Midway through the second half, he collected a pass from Kylian, did a couple of keepie-uppies in the box and then played it back to Paul. His right-foot shot was blocked, so he tried again with his left. *GOAL – 3–1!*

'Yes, Piochi!' Antoine cheered.

Was that game over? Just in case Croatia were planning an incredible comeback, Kylian made sure with a stunning long-range strike. *4–1!*

'Yes, Kyky!' Antoine screamed.

When the full-time whistle blew, he threw his arms up triumphantly. His Euro 2016 heartache was finally over because now, France were the 2018 World Cup winners!

Even after a tiring tournament, the players still had the energy to run around the pitch hugging each other. What an amazing and emotional moment! What a big team effort! Antoine wiped away his tears with his shirt, but this time, they were tears of pure joy.

'We did it!' he told his best friend, Paul. 'We made the French people proud!'

They could hear the celebrations in the stadium in Russia, and they could picture the scenes back home in Paris. Crowds of fans all around the Eiffel Tower, cheering and waving their flags. And it was all because of them.

The Best Player of the Tournament award went

MATT AND TOM OLDFIELD

to Croatia's captain Luka Modrić, but Antoine was named the Man of the Match in the World Cup final. It went nicely with his winners' medal and soon, he would be lifting the greatest prize of all...

Hugo stood in the middle of the French squad, with the World Cup trophy in his hands. 'Ready?' he called out. '3, 2, 1...'

'Hurraaaaaaaaay!!!!' everyone roared.

Campeones, Campeones, Olé! Olé! Olé!

It hadn't been an easy journey for Antoine at all, but thanks to a marvellous mix of talent and determination, he had made it all the way to the top. He had achieved his World Cup dream and he had a simple message for all the clubs that had rejected him as a boy, for all the ones who had said he was too small to be a star.

'Look at me now!'

CHAPTER 2

FOOTBALL-MAD
IN MÂCON

Zinedine Zidane was from Marseille, Thierry Henry
was from Paris, and Youri Djorkaeff was from Lyon.
But what about Mâcon? Which of France's famous
footballers had grown up there?

Back in the 1990s, the answer was none. Mâcon
was a small, quiet, old town on the east side of
France, an hour's drive north of Djorkaeff's Lyon.
Nothing much happened in Mâcon, least of all
sporting success. It had a rugby team and a football
team, but neither was particularly good. The local
people preferred water sports like rowing, swimming
and speedboating.

'Boring!' decided one blond, football-mad boy in

Mâcon. Antoine Griezmann was going to change his town's sporting history forever. From the first moment that he kicked a ball, he fell in love with the beautiful game.

'GOAL!' his dad, Alain, cheered as his three-year-old son ran up and whacked it as hard as he could with his little left foot.

The mini football flew through the air, over the halfway line of the local basketball court, bounced down and then rolled towards the base of the hoop at the other end.

'GOAL!' young Antoine repeated, clapping his tiny hands together. 'Again, again!'

Now that he'd started, there was no stopping him. Antoine was like a puppy with a stick. Each time, he chased after the ball and brought it back to have another go at kicking it.

'Shall we stop for lunch now?' Alain asked after a while. He could hear his stomach rumbling loudly. 'Mummy will be waiting for us and you must be hungry after all that exercise! Don't worry, we can come back and play this afternoon.'

Antoine shook his head stubbornly. 'Again, again!'

'Fine, five more kicks, okay?'

Soon, Alain decided to put up wooden goals to create a proper pitch for his football-mad son. When he saw them, Antoine beamed brightly. Now, he would be able to do less chasing, and more kicking!

'GOAL! GOAL! GOAL!'

As he got older, Antoine did play basketball on that court too, but football was almost always his first-choice sport. At the weekends, he spent hours kicking a ball around with his friends from Les Gautriats, the neighbourhood where the Griezmanns lived. If for some strange reason, they were all busy, Antoine could usually persuade a family member to come out and play goalkeeper.

'Right, that's enough,' his elder sister, Maud, would say after a few shots whizzed past her. 'I'm bored now!'

Antoine shook his head stubbornly. 'Come on, I'm only just getting started!'

'Fine, five more kicks, okay?'

And if for some even stranger reason, none of his

family wanted to play either, Antoine would just practise his football skills on his own. He became the King of the Keepie Uppies –

...*forty-seven, forty-eight, forty-nine, FIFTY, fifty-one...*

– and the Wizard of the One-Touch Pass.

Left foot, right foot, left foot, right foot...

Even on the coldest, wettest winter nights, Antoine would be out there in front of his house, in a rain-soaked shirt, kicking the ball against the garage door again and again.

BANG! THUD!

'Right, that's enough noise for one day,' his mum, Isabelle, would call out eventually from the doorway. 'If you don't stop now, the neighbours will call the police!'

Antoine shook his head stubbornly. No, if he stopped now, he would never become a superstar. He had to keep practising. 'Please Mum, just a little bit longer!'

'Fine, five more kicks, okay?'

Antoine just couldn't get enough. His life was

football, football, and more football. It was the only subject that he was interested in.Every morning at George Brassens Primary School, he sat there doodling football cartoons in his exercise books and waiting for the break-time bell to ring. Why? Football!

'Let's play!' Antoine called to his friends as they rushed out of the classroom door.

And every afternoon, he sat there doodling football cartoons in his exercise books and waiting for the home-time bell to ring. Why? Football!

After racing back to drop off his school bag and grab a quick snack, he was ready to go again.

'Let's play!'

Some evenings, he rushed over to the local court for a kickaround with his mates.

And on other evenings, he rushed off to training sessions with his first football club, Entente Charnay-Mâcon 71.

Antoine just couldn't get enough. His life was football, football, and more football. It was the only subject that he was interested in.

CHAPTER 3

MÂCON'S LITTLE MAGICIAN

Entente Charnay-Mâcon 71 was like a second home for Antoine. He was a familiar face at his local football club long before he even started training with the Under-7s. His dad was the coach of the Under-13s, and so he often went along and stood on the sidelines with him.

'My assistant,' Alain liked to call Antoine.

Antoine did like watching football and learning new skills, but playing the game itself was much more exciting. After a few minutes on the sidelines, he usually got bored and wandered off in search of adventure. He soon knew every corner and every cupboard of the club, and the contents of every cupboard too.

'Where did you get that from?' Alain asked when a football magically appeared at his son's feet.

Antoine shrugged. 'I found it behind the goal,' he lied.

His dad just nodded and went back to coaching. He knew that with a football at his feet, his son would be happily occupied for hours.

By the age of five, Antoine was already training with the Mâcon Under-7s. He loved it and never missed a single minute. The activities were really fun and he could feel himself improving: his touch, his passing, his dribbling, his shooting. Everything! However, practice just wasn't the same as playing proper matches.

'When can I make my debut for Mâcon?' Antoine asked his coach for the fiftieth time.

Bruno Chetoux sighed. It didn't seem fair that a boy who wanted to play couldn't play, but the rules were the rules.

'I'm sorry, kid, but you're still not old enough,' he replied. 'You'll be able to play soon, I promise!'

In the end, Antoine made his debut before
he turned six. There were two reasons for that.
Firstly, Bruno couldn't bear to say no any longer,
and secondly, Antoine was just too talented to be
left out.

In training, he was running rings around everyone.
Once Antoine had the ball, no-one could get it off
him. He could dribble past defenders so easily, like
they were just cones on the ground. There was only
ever one ending – GOAL!

'We need him in our team,' Bruno decided
eventually, '*NOW!*'

'At last!' Antoine cried out when his coach told
him the great news. 'Thanks, I can't wait, it's going
to be amazing!'

He was already imagining all of the goals that
he would score himself, and also all of the goals he
would set up for his teammates.

The strikers were thinking, 'Brilliant, Antoine's
going to create so many chances for us!'

And the defenders were thinking, 'Brilliant, other
teams will have to try and tackle Antoine now, rather

than us!'

Fortunately, Antoine lived up to all their expectations. Suddenly, with their new little magician on the left-wing, Mâcon were unstoppable.

Antoine was having the time of his life out there on the football field. It was like having a kickaround on the basketball court with his mates, only a million times better! He had his very own navy-blue football shirt and he had a crowd to entertain with his skills and celebrations.

'Come on, close the blond boy down!' opposition coaches called out as Antoine set off on another mazy dribble. 'Stop him, STOP HIM!'

But as hard as they tried, they couldn't – *GOAL!*

As Antoine slid across the mud on his knees, the spectators talked excitedly about him:

'Wow, that boy's a bit special!'

'What a lovely left-foot!'

Antoine made football look so easy, but as Bruno wondered: was it *too* easy for him? Before long, the coach moved his new star player up to the next age group. Would he be able to shine so brightly against bigger, older boys?

Yes, it turned out. Even at a higher level, Antoine was still Mâcon's little magician. His new team won match after match after match. First, they conquered the local region, and then they travelled further and further to find better teams to beat. Different city, same result. In fact, Antoine got so used to winning that when he didn't, he was absolutely devastated.

'H-how did we l-lose that?' he spluttered tearfully as his dad drove him home.

'These things happen sometimes,' Alain explained. Of course, he wanted to comfort his upset son, but it was also an important lesson for him to learn. 'I know it's not a nice feeling to lose, but we can't win all the time.'

Antoine nodded and wiped away his tears with his shirt. Before long, his champion spirit had returned. Next week, he thought, he would do whatever he could to get his team back to winning ways.

CHAPTER 4

FOOTBALL IN THE FAMILY

'Mum, can Theo come and play football with us today?' Antoine asked one afternoon as he got ready to go out to the court.

Isabelle frowned. 'I don't think so, darling. Not today.'

Her youngest son was still only two years old, and not yet ready for the hustle and bustle of big kid football. It was sweet that Antoine wanted to play with his baby brother, but he would have to find another, older goalkeeper.

'Please!' Antoine begged. 'Don't worry, it'll just be the three of us – me, Maud and Theo. We'll look after him, I promise!'

'Fine, but only for half an hour, okay? And if Theo starts crying, bring him home straight away.'

'Yes, Mum! Thanks, Mum!'

As the three young Griezmanns walked over to the basketball court, Antoine tried to explain the plan to his little brother.

'Today, Theo, we're going to teach you how to play football! What do you think about that?'

His younger brother giggled away.

'He certainly seems excited!' Maud laughed.

As Antoine took up his position in goal, she placed the ball in front of Theo's foot, just like their dad had done for them.

'Ready, steady, KICK!'

Theo swung his leg wildly but somehow the ball bounced and rolled towards the goal. Antoine had a save to make but he knew what he was supposed to do next. He wanted his baby brother to love football too, after all. With a dramatic dive, he let Theo's shot slip straight through his hands.

'Noooooooo!' Antoine groaned, putting on his best acting performance ever.

'GOAL!' cheered Maud.

'GOAL!' young Theo repeated, clapping his tiny hands together. 'Again, again!'

Antoine smiled at his sister. His plan had worked perfectly. 'Great, it looks like we've got another footballer in the family!'

The minutes flew by until Maud checked her watch and panicked. They were going to be late!

'Right, home-time,' she called out. 'Come on, quickly you two!'

After a happy half-hour of dramatic dives and 'GOAL!'s, Theo's first football session was over. They couldn't wait to tell their mum all about it.

'Theo is so good at football already!' Antoine announced eagerly as soon as he walked through the front door. 'He loved scoring lots of goals, didn't he, Maud?'

'Yeah, the only time he cried was when we took the ball away at the end!'

Isabelle laughed. 'Good, I'm glad you had a nice time together. Maybe we'll soon have three more footballers in the family!'

Antoine was confused. Their dad was a football *coach*, but he wasn't a football *player*. 'What do you mean "three *more*", Mum?'

'Well, my dad – your grandad – was a footballer too, remember!'

'Oh yeah, how did I forget that!'

Their grandad, Amaro Lopes, was now pretty old but as a young man growing up in Portugal, he had been a big, strong defender for his local club, FC Paços de Ferreira. His career ended when he moved to France, but he still had photos of his glorious footballing days.

'That's me right there,' he said, proudly showing Antoine one picture. 'Look, I'm almost as tall as our goalkeeper!'

'I hope I grow up to be as tall as you!'

'I'm sure you will!'

Sometimes, the Griezmann family spent their summer holidays back in Paços de Ferreira. Antoine got to visit the FC Paços de Ferreira stadium and watch a match. The team were now playing in the country's top league, against famous clubs like

Porto and Sporting Lisbon.

'Perhaps, you'll play football for Portugal one day!' Amaro said hopefully.

Portugal? Antoine thought for a moment. The 1998 World Cup had changed everything for him. Not only had France won the trophy for the first time ever by beating Ronaldo's Brazil, but Antoine had got the chance to meet all the players before their group game against Denmark.

What a day that had been! Wearing a France shirt with '7' on the back, he ran around excitedly with his best friend Jean-Baptiste, getting all the stars to sign his football: Thierry Henry, Bixente Lizarazu, Fabien Barthez, Robert Pires, Christian Karembeu and, best of all, Zinedine Zidane. Those guys were his new heroes now.

So, when Amaro asked him if he might play for Portugal, he replied firmly. 'Sorry Grandad, I can't. I'm going to play for *Les Bleus!*'

CHAPTER 5

UF MÂCONNAIS

As eight-year-old Antoine prepared to take his next step towards becoming a French superstar, Mâcon made a very important change to their football system. Instead of three different clubs, there would now be just one: Union du Football Mâconnais, or UF Mâconnais for short.

How many youth teams would they have? Would there be enough space for everyone? Many youngsters were worried, but not Antoine. He knew that he was good enough to star for Mâcon's new super-club.

'It's going to be great,' he told Jean-Baptiste. 'Now, we'll get the chance to beat even better teams!'

As part of the big change, UF Mâconnais had

moved up to France's fifth division. That was a higher level than he had ever played at before, but Antoine was ready to rise to the challenge. He was still very small and skinny for his age but what he lacked in size, he made up for in spirit. No-one was more desperate to become a professional footballer than the blond boy from Les Gautriats.

'I'm going to make it!' Antoine kept telling himself, and he never stopped believing.

He worked extra hard on the things that he was really good at, like dribbling, passing, and crossing. And he also worked extra hard on the things that he wasn't so good at, like shooting, tackling, and heading. He didn't care that he was the smallest member of the Under-11s; he still wanted to be the best at heading.

At the UF Mâconnais senior team's home games, the junior players sometimes took part in the half-time show. Antoine loved running out onto the pitch with so many faces watching him. It felt like he was a superstar already.

'Jump!' the coaches shouted as they put crosses

into the box. The UF Mâconnais youngsters lined up and took it in turns to try and head the ball into the net.

As Antoine leapt high into the air, he watched the cross carefully. It was coming towards him at top speed, but he had to be brave.

'This is it!' he thought to himself. He imagined that it was the last minute of a big cup final and this was his chance to score the winner and become a hero. Antoine used his neck muscles to put extra power on the header, just like his coach had taught him.

Gooooooooooooooooooooaaaaaaaaaaaaaaaalllllllllllll llllllllllllll!!!!!!!!!!!!!!!!!!!!

For a second, Antoine forgot that he wasn't really playing in a cup final. He turned and threw his arms up in the air triumphantly. Then it hit him: oh yeah, he had made that part up!

'Hey, you do know that you're not Zidane, right?' Jean-Baptiste teased him.

Antoine smiled back. 'Not yet, no, but I will be soon!'

By the time he turned ten, he was already

training with the UF Mâconnais Under-13s. Their coach, Christophe Grosjean, had seen Antoine in action many times over the years, but watching him up close at practice, he was more impressed than ever.

In terms of technique, Antoine was untouchable. With the ball at his feet, he could do things that not even Christophe's twelve-year-olds could do. He glided across the grass with the balance, control, and grace of... well, a superstar!

Everyone loved watching Antoine dribble down the wing. It was so exciting. What would he do next? If defenders weren't careful, he quickly made them look like fools. Sometimes, Antoine showed off tricks that he had spent hours learning at home, but a lot of the time, it was just his natural talent shining through.

'When he grows a bit,' Christophe thought to himself, 'he's going to be sensational!'

That was Antoine's only issue; he was still so small and weak for his age. Yes, he had silky skills, but what use was that when big defenders could muscle him off the ball so easily?

'Foul!' he cried out in frustration at first, but his Under-13s coach just shook his head. 'Play on!'

Antoine didn't argue; he just picked himself up and chased after the ball again. Christophe could see that the UF Mâconnais players were being careful with their teammate; real opponents would kick and push him all over the pitch. No, he couldn't let that happen.

'So, when do I get to make my debut?' Antoine asked eagerly one day. He loved the training sessions, but they just weren't the same as playing proper matches.

'Sorry, kid,' Christophe replied as kindly as possible. 'We don't think you're ready just yet.'

Instead, the coach sent Antoine back down to the Under-12s for the rest of the season. Antoine was devastated. It felt like a big step backwards.

'It's so boring here!' he sulked for the first few days but before long, his champion spirit returned. There was only one way to prove Christophe wrong:

Goooooooooooooooooooooaaaaaaaaaaaaaaaaaallllllllllll

IIIIIIIIIIIIIII!!!!!!!!!!!!!!!!!!!!

Gooooooooooooooooooooaaaaaaaaaaaaaaaaaallllllllllll

IIIIIIIIIIIIIII!!!!!!!!!!!!!!!!!!!!

Gooooooooooooooooooooaaaaaaaaaaaaaaaaaallllllllllll

IIIIIIIIIIIIIIIII!!!!!!!!!!!!!!!!!!!!!!

A few months later, Antoine was called up to the Under-13s squad again. By then, he was a little taller, a lot tougher, and all set to become a superstar.

'Welcome back!' Christophe said with a smile. He could feel the boy's confidence, burning like a beacon. 'Those defenders don't stand a chance now!'

CHAPTER 6

FOOTBALL DREAMS
WITH FRIENDS

The UF Mâconnais youth players were best friends, both on and off the field. Antoine, Jean-Baptiste, Stéphane, Julian and Martin – the boys spent almost all their spare time together. And what was the bond that united them? Football!

On the few weekends when they weren't playing for the Under-13s, they met up to play FIFA on the PlayStation, swap Panini stickers...

Got, got, NEED!

...and, of course, play football. By then, Antoine had mostly left the basketball court near his home behind. He only went there when his brother Theo wanted to practice his shooting. Antoine needed more space for his deadly dribbles and a proper, grass pitch too. Why? So, that he could celebrate his goals by doing awesome knee-slides!

The summer of 2002 was a World Cup summer and they all had their favourite players.

'Today, I'm going to be Thierry Henry!'

'I'll be Zidane!'

'I'll be Ronaldo!

'Oh, I wanted to be him. Fine, I'll be Raúl instead!'

'Okay, who am I?' Jean-Baptiste asked and then started to dance. The others were soon rolling around on the floor laughing.

'Mate, what on earth was THAT?' Stéphane asked. 'Don't ever do that again; it was the worst dance I've ever seen!'

Antoine knew his stuff, though. He guessed the right answer straight away: 'Papa Bouba Diop!'

'See!' Jean-Baptiste beamed happily. 'At least someone's been watching the World Cup!'

Antoine had watched every minute of every match. So, who would he choose to be? He was a huge France fan, but Henry and Zidane were already taken. He was a big fan of the Juventus midfielder, Pavel Nedvěd, but he wasn't playing because the Czech Republic hadn't qualified.

Luckily, Antoine had one last hero he could choose: his greatest hero of all, David Beckham.

'I'll be Becks!' he called out.

Antoine wanted to bend the ball just like Beckham, only with his left foot instead of his right. He spent hours watching videos of his hero's greatest passes, crosses and, best of all, free kicks. There were so many of them:

For Manchester United against Liverpool and West Ham and Barcelona,

And for England against Columbia and Mexico and Greece.

The power, the curl, the accuracy – it was absolutely amazing! 'How does Becks do it?' Antoine marvelled.

And it wasn't just his football skills that Antoine admired. It was his style too – the cool clothes, the classy photos, and the ever-changing haircuts.

Antoine tried his best to copy Becks. His parents

didn't always let him have the latest haircut, but he wore a long-sleeved shirt with the number '7' on the back. That made him feel like Beckham, but could he play like Beckham?

Yes, he could! As he dribbled forward, he looked up and spotted Julian racing down the right wing. It was time to be Becks! In a flash, he pulled back his left leg and played a perfect long-range pass to his teammate. *GOAL!*

'Thanks, Becks!'

'No problem, *Zizou!* '

Their games went on and on, often all day long. If someone had to go home, they could usually find another local kid ready to replace them.

'Right, Robert is on your team now!'

There were only four things that could make their matches end:

1) hunger,

2) heavy rain or snow,

3) darkness, and

4) angry mums and dads.

That particular day, it was darkness that stopped them.

'Okay, next goal wins!' Martin called out as the last of the sunlight disappeared.

'What? That's not fair – our team is winning by four goals!' Jean-Baptiste complained. They were all best friends but once they stepped out onto the football pitch, all that changed – a competitive edge came into play.

'No, you're not!'

'Yes, we are!'

'It's 37–35!'

'No, it's 38–34! That goal didn't count, remember, because Jacques handballed it. And then we scored that one where—'

'Hey, it doesn't matter,' Antoine interrupted. 'Let's just play on and make sure that we score the next goal.'

'Fine,' Jean-Baptiste muttered moodily.

He passed to Antoine who dribbled forward at top speed, past one opponent, then another, then—

'FOUL!' he cried out as he fell to the floor.

'No way, you dived!' Martin argued. 'I won the ball fair and square, and you know it, Becks!'

Antoine wasn't backing down this time. 'As if, Henry! That tackle was worse than that one you did against Uruguay!'

What they really needed was a referee, but eventually, the decision went Antoine's way. *Free kick!*

It was the last minute of the 2002 World Cup Final. This was it – his chance to be the hero. Antoine closed his eyes, took a deep breath, and focused on being Becks.

'Come on, get on with it!' Stéphane shouted. 'We haven't got all night!'

Antoine ran up and struck the ball powerfully, with plenty of curl. It whizzed past the players in the wall and past the goalkeeper too.

Goooooooooooooooooooaaaaaaaaaaaaaaaallllllllllll lllllllllllll!!!!!!!!!!!!!!!!!!!

Becks had done it; he had won the World Cup! Antoine punched the air and then performed another awesome knee-slide.

CHAPTER 7

TOO SMALL TO BE A STAR?

Antoine got older and a little bit taller, but his life dream always stayed the same. At school, whenever he was asked what job he wanted to do in the future, he wrote down two wonderful words:

'Professional Footballer.'

'It's great to have that ambition,' his teachers told him, 'but it's a very, very competitive world. It's best to have other options too. There are lots of other interesting careers out there. What else do you like doing?'

Playing football, though, was all Antoine had ever wanted to do. He knew that it wouldn't be easy, but he was willing to work and work until he reached his target. Nothing was going to stop him, and especially not his size.

However, that was more of an issue than ever. Antoine was still a small thirteen-year-old and at that age, French kids switched from playing in smaller nine-a-side spaces to playing on great big eleven-a-side pitches. Suddenly, there was so much space everywhere. It was like taking a tiny goldfish out of its tank and dropping it in the Atlantic Ocean!

Antoine did his best to show off his silky skills as usual, but his little legs couldn't last the whole match. All that running was really exhausting. When the new UF Mâconnais coach, Jean Belver, saw how much he was struggling, he dropped him down to the bench instead.

'Don't worry, you'll get your chance to shine in the second half,' Belver told him.

Antoine *was* worried, though. Being a substitute was unbearable! He couldn't imagine anything worse than sitting there watching as his best friends left him behind. Jean-Baptiste, Stéphane, Martin, Julian

– they were all out there having fun on the football pitch without him.

'I need to get back into the starting line-up!' Antoine told himself through gritted teeth. There was only one way to prove Belver wrong, the next time he got on a pitch:

Goooooooooooooooooooooaaaaaaaaaaaaaaaaallllllllllll llllllllllllll!!!!!!!!!!!!!!!!!!!

'I'M BACK!' Antoine roared, celebrating with another awesome knee-slide.

At UF Mâconnais, everyone knew Antoine well, and they had full faith in his character. After all, their little blond magician had shown his special champion spirit by bouncing back time and time again. There was no problem whatsoever with his mental strength, and he was working hard to improve his physical strength too.

'Just keep doing what you're doing,' the coach encouraged his left-wing wizard. 'You'll get your growth spurt soon, I'm sure!'

Unfortunately, not everyone shared Belver's belief. During the 2004–05 season, Alain took his son to trials at lots of top clubs all across France. It turned out to be a very tough experience for Antoine.

First, Antoine had a trial for his favourite team, Olympique Lyonnais. It was the closest big club to Mâcon, and he had been a fan ever since his dad took him to his first match at the Stade de Gerland. The adventure, the action, the atmosphere – it was by far the best experience of his life.

'I'm going to play for Lyon when I'm older!' he announced afterwards.

Antoine's favourite player was their Brazilian striker, Sonny Anderson, and amazingly, he got the chance to meet his hero. He was too star-struck to say very much, but he proudly put the photo up on his bedroom wall, next to his posters of Nedvěd, Zidane and Beckham.

So, he was full of excitement when he arrived at the training ground to start his trial. He couldn't wait to become the next Sonny Anderson.

'Hi, Didier! Hi, François!'

Antoine knew most of the Lyon youth coaches already because he attended the club's training

camps every summer. They, of course, knew him too
– his strengths *and* his weaknesses.

Alain Duthéron was one scout at Lyon who had
been keeping a close eye on Antoine for years.
Duthéron loved the boy's style, but unfortunately,
Antoine's size was still a big problem. At that time,
French clubs just weren't looking for small, skilful
players; they wanted tall, powerful players. As
talented as he was, Antoine didn't fit that description
at all.

'I know, but that boy is *special!*' said Duthéron,
doing his best to persuade the Lyon youth coaches
to be patient with Antoine, but they wouldn't
listen. The boy's parents were small too; there was
no chance that he would grow up to be big and
strong.

'No' – that one short word hurt like a wound, like
a punch in the gut. Antoine was devastated, but he
picked himself up and carried on.

'There are plenty of other clubs out there,' his
dad reassured him, and after one rejection, Antoine
wasn't just going to give up. He was determined to

achieve his life dream of becoming a professional footballer. No matter what.

Antoine would have to keep reminding himself of that, because there were more hard times ahead.

He was invited to a trial at AS Saint-Étienne, but it was cancelled due to snow.

'We'll try again next time,' his dad said.

He went on trial at FC Sochaux, but like Lyon, they decided that he was too small to be a star.

'We'll try again next time,' his dad said.

He went on trial at AJ Auxerre, but when they took an X-ray of his wrist to predict his future height, the results weren't good. No, they told him, he would always be too small to be a star.

'We'll try again next time,' his dad said.

By then, Antoine really felt like walking away from football, but he didn't. Instead, he went on trial at FC Metz and this time, the club seemed interested in signing him. Finally, was his football dream about to come true? But just when his hopes were up, he heard the same old story:

'Sorry, we think you're too small to be a star.'

Not again! Antoine was too upset to say anything, so his dad spoke up instead.

'You really think my son is too small?' Alain asked angrily. 'Well, we'll see about that!'

How could they say that about Antoine when he was still so young? Kids often didn't get their growth spurt until they were fifteen or sixteen!

'We'll try again next time,' his dad said.

Really? Could Antoine deal with any more disappointments? Fortunately, he wouldn't have to.

CHAPTER 8

SCOUTED BY SOCIEDAD

In Summer 2005, Real Sociedad scout Éric Olhats decided to stop in Paris on his way back from Argentina. He had some football friends in the city who he wanted to catch up with. For Éric, it was just a small change of plan. For Antoine, however, it would turn out to be a life-changing decision.

Montpellier HSC were the latest French club who had offered him a trial. Their scout Manu Christophe was a big fan of Antoine's silky skills, but their youth coach Christophe Blondeau wasn't so sure. The problem? His size, of course.

'Okay, well let's take him to the international tournament,' they agreed. 'It'll be the perfect way to test how good he really is!'

Alain drove Antoine all the way to Montpellier to meet up with his new teammates. Carrying the club kit in his hands, he boarded the bus heading to Paris.

'Good luck, son!' his dad called out through the car window.

Antoine was excited about playing in such a big tournament, but he wasn't getting his hopes up. After his Metz disappointment, he knew that anything could go wrong. Anything! He might sit on the bench all day, or Montpellier might lose every match and go home early...

'No, I've got to stay positive,' Antoine told himself as he stared out of the bus window. 'I can do this!'

*

That day, Éric's football friends were watching an Under-15s tournament at the Paris Saint-Germain training ground, so he went along to join them. He didn't usually scout youth players for Sociedad but if there was a game going on, he would keep his eyes open for top talent. Éric was a professional, after all.

'Have you spotted anyone special?' he asked his

friends.

'Not yet!' they replied hopefully.

The matches were short and played at top speed. The action was end-to-end like a tennis match. Every young player was in a hurry to become the next football hero.

'Slow down and think!' Éric wanted to shout to them, but he didn't.

Eventually, the Real Sociedad scout saw a kid who had the right idea. The little left-winger for Montpellier was a joy to watch. As he dribbled forward, he looked so composed on the ball, like he had all the time in the world.

'That's more like it!'

The more Éric watched, the more interested he became. The blond boy was nowhere near as strong as the other players, but he was easily the best footballer on the pitch. Surely, that was the thing that mattered most?

'When he grows a bit,' the scout thought to himself, 'he's going to be sensational!'

Éric was desperate to know more about the

Montpellier left-winger.

'Is that little blond boy your son?' he asked the parents on the sidelines, but they all shook their heads.

So, Éric went to speak to the Montpellier coach instead. After some small talk, he moved on to the most important topic.

'Your winger has a lovely left foot,' Éric said, attempting to sound as casual as possible.

'Antoine? Yes, he's a very talented kid,' Blondeau admitted. 'He's on trial at the moment but sadly we won't be signing him. He's just not what we're looking for right now.'

Éric nodded, trying his best to hold back the smile that was spreading across his face. The scout's mind was made up; he was going to ask Antoine to come to Real Sociedad.

But how? And when? He couldn't do anything without speaking to the boy's parents first, and they weren't there at the tournament.

Like Antoine, Éric wasn't someone who gave up easily. He called the Sociedad Sporting Director, Roberto Olabe, and told him the story of

Montpellier's little magician.

'What should I do?' the scout asked.

Olabe's reply was short and simple: 'Just invite the boy to come here for a trial.'

So, during a break between matches, Éric walked over and handed him a folded piece of paper. He had written a message on the top: 'Don't open this until you get home!'

Antoine read it, smiled and nodded. 'Thanks, I won't!'

*

What else was written on that piece of paper? That was the question going around and around Antoine's brain on the long journey back to Montpellier. He held the note tightly in his hand, but he kept his promise to Éric. He didn't look until he was back home with his family.

'Open it! Open it!' Theo chanted impatiently.

'Okay, okay!' Antoine said, unfolding the page at last. As he read it to himself silently, his hands began to shake.

'What does it say?' Maud asked. 'Read it aloud!'

Antoine cleared his throat and then began. 'We would like to invite you to come to Spain for a trial at Real Sociedad.'

'Congratulations! Anything else?'

'There's a name and a phone number at the bottom.'

'Éric Olhats' – soon, the man would feel like part of the Griezmann family. But at first, Antoine's parents were worried.

'I'll call the scout tomorrow,' Alain said cautiously. He just didn't want his son to suffer another disappointment like Metz. 'We'll need to know all the details first.'

'Yes, I'm really not sure about this offer,' Isabelle added. She hated the idea of her son being so far from home. 'Moving to Spain would be a very big step.'

Slowly but surely, however, Éric managed to persuade Antoine's parents to let him go. First, there were long phone calls, and then the scout visited the Griezmann family home. He showed them photos of the Real Sociedad academy and gave them lots of information about schools and training sessions.

'And I'll always be there to look after him,' Éric promised.

Antoine beamed brightly at all the academy pictures. Football in Spain looked awesome, and the best bit was yet to come. Éric had a special gift for him: his first Real Sociedad shirt.

'Cool, thanks!' Antoine said, admiring the shirt's blue and white stripes. He couldn't wait to wear it proudly.

Alain and Isabelle could see how much their son wanted this. How could they say no and dash his dream of becoming a professional footballer?

'Okay, we'll take you to the trial!' they agreed.

Antoine was over the moon. So long, UF Mâconnais – he was setting off on a Spanish adventure!

CHAPTER 9

STAYING STRONG IN SPAIN

Antoine had one trial at Real Sociedad in the spring and then another one in the summer. He really enjoyed both experiences, but had he done enough to impress the youth coach, Iñigo Cortés? Was the club willing to take a chance on a skinny little French kid with a lovely left foot? Yes and yes!

'We'd like to offer Antoine a place at our academy,' Iñigo told the boy's proud parents.

'Thank you, he'll be so happy to hear that!' Alain replied emotionally.

It was the best moment of Antoine's young life, but there would be difficult days ahead. Signing for Sociedad meant moving to Spain and that meant

learning a new language and living a long way
from home. That was an awful lot of change for a
fourteen-year-old to cope with.

'We're going to miss you!' his mum sobbed as they
said their goodbyes at the airport. 'Look after yourself
and call us whenever you want to talk!'

At first, Antoine stayed at a boarding school near
the border between France and Spain, and then
travelled to training every evening. But all that toing
and froing soon left him feeling tired, lonely and
fed up. One day when Éric went to pick him up, he
could see that the boy was very upset.

'What's wrong?' he asked kindly.

Antoine couldn't hold it in any longer. All of a
sudden, he burst into tears. 'I want to go home,' he
managed to say eventually. He wanted to go back to
living with his parents, and Maud and Theo, and to
playing football with Jean-Baptiste and Stéphane.
'I hate that school. I don't have any friends there
and I miss Mâcon!'

Éric comforted Antoine as best he could. He
wasn't the first young boy to feel homesick at

Sociedad. It was only natural.

'Stay strong, kid,' the scout told him. 'Things will get better, I promise!'

Éric had an idea that might help, but he needed to speak to the Sporting Director first. Once Olabe had agreed, Éric asked Antoine, 'Would you like to come and live at my house in Bayonne?'

Bayonne was a French city that was near to the boy's school and also only an hour's drive from San Sebastián, just over the border with Spain and the home of Real Sociedad.

'Yes please!' Antoine agreed eagerly.

Now that they were solving his problems off the pitch, it was time for Antoine to focus *on* the football pitch. With his long blond hair and flashy boots, he arrived at Sociedad looking like a mini mix between Pavel Nedvěd and David Beckham. But did he have the skill to go with the style?

'Just give me the ball and I'll show you!' Antoine said with a cheeky smile. Despite being the new kid in the team, he was full of confidence.

Iñigo liked the confidence and he liked the talent

too. He decided to put Antoine in the older age group alongside Sociedad's two other French players, Jonathan Lupinelli and Lucas Puyol. The coach hoped that would help him to feel at home. The plan worked; the trio were soon inseparable, laughing and joking together in their native language.

The only problem with Iñigo's plan was that Antoine was now the youngest player in the team as well as the smallest. He wasn't just going to walk straight into the starting line-up. He still had lots to learn and a lot of improvements to make.

'That's it, Antoine!' his coach encouraged him. 'Keep going!'

Some days, however, it felt too much like UF Mâconnais all over again. Antoine hadn't moved all the way to Spain just to sit on the Sociedad bench!

'You could always come back and play for us again?' Jean-Baptiste often suggested on the phone.

But as tempting as that sounded, Antoine stayed strong. 'No, I'm not giving up now!' he said determinedly.

During each school holiday, Antoine was

allowed to return to Mâcon for a few weeks of
family, fun and, of course, football with his friends.
But when the time came, he always went back
to Sociedad, with a brave face and a brand new
haircut.

'*Super cool, Grizi!*' Jonathan joked.

For Iñigo and the other Sociedad youth coaches,
Antoine was like an awkward piece in a jigsaw
puzzle. He was clearly a very special playmaker, with
amazing control and creativity, but how could they
fit him into the team? In the end, it was the same
old answer every time:

'First, he has to grow bigger and stronger.'

Antoine tried to be as patient as possible, but that
wasn't easy for a football-mad boy who just wanted
to play the game. One year passed, then another, and
then another...

Was Antoine making any progress at all? It
sometimes felt like his feet were stuck in quicksand.
Often when they called, his parents could hear the
frustration in his voice.

'You know, you can always come home if you

want to,' his mum reminded him.

But as tempting as that sounded, Antoine stayed strong. 'No, I'm not giving up now!' he said determinedly.

Whenever he was feeling low, Antoine talked it through with Éric. That always made him feel better. Éric was always happy to help, whatever the issue. Sometimes, they just sat and chatted about Antoine's life back in Mâcon. And sometimes, they went out onto the football pitch for extra one-on-one training sessions.

Despite all the setbacks, Antoine's passion for his favourite sport never faded. What he lacked in size, he made up for in spirit. He was ready to put in all the hard work necessary to achieve his dream.

'You're going to be great,' Éric reassured him. 'It's only a matter of time before you become a superstar!'

CHAPTER 10

ANTOINE'S BIG BREAKTHROUGH

It was during the 2008–09 season when Antoine really started to shine at Real Sociedad. He was scoring more goals, he was creating more chances, and he was also growing at last. From 5ft 1in, he suddenly shot up to 5ft 9in!

'Where has our lovely little boy gone?' his parents teased him.

And not only was Antoine getting taller, but he was also getting stronger. Finally, he had some extra power out on the pitch and defenders couldn't just push him off the ball. Éric and Iñigo were delighted. That awkward piece of the jigsaw was finally fitting into place!

'There's no stopping him now,' they agreed.

Antoine was still waiting for his big breakthrough moment, though. By the age of eighteen, Becks had been on the verge of making his Manchester United debut. Antoine, on the other hand, still felt far away from the Sociedad first team.

'What can I do to catch Lillo's eye?' he wondered.

Juan Manuel Lillo was the manager of the senior squad, who were struggling down in Spain's Second Division. Scoring goals was their biggest problem, and Antoine could certainly help with that!

Perhaps his big breakthrough would come at Sociedad's famous junior tournament? Becks himself had played there for Manchester United back in the early 1990s. More than fifteen years later, Antoine would get the chance to follow in his hero's footsteps. This time, Sociedad would be competing against Spain's top youth teams, including Barcelona, Valencia and Atlético Madrid.

'Bring it on!' Antoine thought to himself.

All of the Sociedad players were super-excited. The tournament was all they talked about for weeks. Not only would the final take place at the club's main stadium, the Anoeta, but it would also be shown live on Spanish TV.

'Right, we *have* to go all the way and win it!' the youngsters told each other.

First, however, Sociedad had three games in three days against Sevilla, Barcelona, and local rivals Athletic Bilbao. That was an awful lot of football for the Under-19s to play, so their coach, Meho Kodro, had plenty of attacking options to choose from. Would he go with Antoine or Joseba Beitia on the left wing against Sevilla?

When Antoine saw the teamsheet, he punched the air joyfully. 'Thanks, you won't regret this!' he promised his coach.

This was it: Antoine's time to shine. He was going to pay Kodro back with lots of skills and shots…

Goooooooooooooooooooooaaaaaaaaaaaaaaaaaalllllllllllll llllllllllllllll!!!!!!!!!!!!!!!!!!!!!

As the ball rocketed past the Sevilla goalkeeper, Antoine threw his arms up in the air and then slid across the grass on his knees.

'Come on!' he roared.

Antoine was off the mark and suddenly his confidence was sky-high. He scored four more against Bilbao and Barcelona. A new Sociedad star was born, and they were through to the final!

'We always knew you had the talent,' Kodro said with a big smile, 'and now you're really making the most of it!'

Sociedad's opponents at the Anoeta would be Atlético Madrid. With the TV cameras watching, could Antoine add to his five goals and become the hero in the biggest game of all?

Not quite, but he never stopped creating chances for his team. Sociedad took the lead, but Atlético equalised in the last few minutes. Although it was very disappointing, there was no time to despair. The Sociedad players had to lift themselves for the penalty shoot-out!

'Heads up, lads,' Kodro clapped and cheered. 'We can still win this!'

The tension was unbearable. Antoine could hardly watch as, one by one, his teammates stepped up to the spot. He felt sick with the suspense...

GOAL!

'Nice one, Jon!'

GOAL!

'Great strike, Iñigo!'

Eventually, their goalkeeper, Alex Ruiz, dived low to save the day. 4–3 – Real Sociedad were the winners!

'Yessssssssss!' Antoine screamed as he and his teammates raced over to celebrate with their spot-kick hero. Even winning the World Cup couldn't feel much better than this.

Campeones, Campeones, Olé! Olé! Olé!

Out on the Anoeta pitch, there were hugs and songs, and then medals and trophies. Antoine didn't win the Best Player award, but he did pick up the prize for Top Scorer. What a terrific tournament it had been for him! This was the big breakthrough that he'd been waiting for.

So, what next for Sociedad's new star? Antoine signed a new contract at the club and for the rest of the season, he carried on starring for the Under-19s,

and trying to catch Lillo's eye. Although that
didn't happen, there was soon a new Sociedad
manager to impress. Martín Lasarte's task was to
take the club back up to La Liga, and how was
he going to do that? By giving the youngsters
a chance.

Back home in Uruguay, Lasarte had kick-started
the career of an eighteen-year-old forward called…
Luis Suárez! Could he help Antoine to become the
'next big thing'?

The new Sociedad manager wanted to have at
least two players fighting for every position. It didn't
matter how old they were, as long as they had the
right attitude and the right amount of talent.

Goalkeepers? Tick!

Defenders? Tick!

Central midfielders? Tick!

Right-wingers? Tick!

Strikers? Tick!

There was just one gap that still needed to be
filled.

'What I'm looking for is a tricky left winger,'

Lasarte told the youth coaches. 'Do you have anyone who fits the bill?'

'Yes, we do!' they replied eagerly.

What a stroke of luck! Aged eighteen, Antoine skipped straight past the Reserves and started training with the Sociedad first team.

CHAPTER 11

A SUCCESSFUL
START

The first training session with the first-team is a scary
moment for any footballer. To some, it feels like being
thrown in at the deep end of a pool full of sharks and
told to sink or swim.

PANIC!

Not Antoine, though. He had already showed his
strong character time and time again to bounce back
from rejections and setbacks. He wasn't going to
let nerves or youth get in the way of achieving his
dream. He was so close now.

'Everyone, this is Antoine,' Lasarte announced to
the Sociedad squad. 'He'll be joining us for the next
few weeks.'

The older, more experienced players looked across at the young left-winger and grunted. No, they weren't just going to welcome the latest wonderkid with open arms. In fact, quite the opposite; they were going to test his talent and, most importantly, his resilience. Antoine would have to work hard to earn his place in the team.

'Bring it on!' he told himself.

It didn't take long for him to impress Lasarte with his attitude. The Sociedad manager was looking for a determined team player, and Antoine ticked all the right boxes.

For such a skilful player, he wasn't selfish. If a striker was in a better position to score, Antoine always passed.

And for such a skinny player, he wasn't weak. In practice, he battled bravely against the big Sociedad defenders and if he got knocked down, he got straight back up again.

Lasarte liked everything about Antoine. The Sociedad attack needed something a little different, but was the eighteen-year-old ready to be their creative spark? There was only one way to find out – by giving him game-time in the pre-season friendlies.

The manager brought Antoine on for the second half against CD Anaitasuna. From the first time he touched the ball until the final whistle, Antoine dribbled forward with freedom and flair. The poor defenders didn't know what to do to stop him. He twisted and turned his way through and then finished things off with his lethal left foot.

Goooooooooooooooooooooaaaaaaaaaaaaaaaaaallllllllllllll llllllllllllllll!!!!!!!!!!!!!!!!!!!

Goooooooooooooooooooooaaaaaaaaaaaaaaaaaallllllllllllll llllllllllllllll!!!!!!!!!!!!!!!!!!!

What a debut! Antoine was certainly catching the eye, but could he keep it up? Yes, he could! He scored two more in the next match against FC Barakaldo, and then another against SD Eibar.

Just like at the junior tournament, Antoine had taken his chances spectacularly. With five goals in his first four games, he was quickly becoming the talk of the town.

*'What do you know about this new wonderkid?
"Griezmann" – is he German?'*

*'No, I'm pretty sure he's French. I really don't
know much about him, other than that he's got a
lovely left foot!'*

Antoine was loving his new life in the Sociedad
first team. His manager believed in him and he had
passed his teammates' test – he was one of the lads
now.

'If you nutmeg me one more time, Grizi, you'll be
sorry!' joked the right-back, Carlos Martínez.

'You'll have to catch me first!' Antoine called back
cheekily.

He felt ready to be Sociedad's creative spark in the
Second Division, but not everyone agreed about that.

'Lots of kids play well in preseason,' some argued,
'but that doesn't mean anything. Remember, he's
only eighteen! It's way too soon for him to start in
the league.'

When the 2009–10 season kicked off, Antoine had
to watch from the sidelines, but he didn't stay there
long. Sociedad only won one out of their first four

GRIEZMANN

matches, and the fans quickly became frustrated.

'Give Griezmann a go!' they cried out.

Lasarte listened carefully. It was time to see what their young star could do. Antoine came on as a late sub in the Spanish Cup against Rayo Vallecano, and then in the league against Real Murcia, and Gimnàstic, and Girona...

'Come on, Griezmann should be starting!' the Sociedad supporters complained.

Again, Lasarte listened carefully. At home at the Anoeta, he picked Antoine to make his full league debut against SD Huesca.

Antoine couldn't wait to play more minutes. He might not last the full ninety, but he was going to create as many goalscoring chances as possible. He wanted to excite, entertain and, of course, win. His family would all be there to watch him, after all.

'Are you ready for this?' his strike partner, Imanol Agirretxe asked as the two teams lined up in the tunnel.

'You bet I am!' Antoine replied confidently. He could already hear the noise of the crowd, and he wanted to give them something to cheer even louder about.

For the first thirty minutes, Antoine struggled to get into the game. All of Sociedad's attacks were going down the right wing.

'Over here!' he kept calling for the ball, in acres of space on the left.

Finally, Antoine got the pass that he wanted. Right, it was his time to shine, and he had a clever plan. The Huesca defenders already knew about his lovely left foot, but did they also know about his brilliant right?

Not yet! Antoine cut inside and fired off a quick shot that caught everyone by surprise. The ball zoomed powerfully past the goalkeeper and into the bottom corner.

Goooooooooooooooooooooaaaaaaaaaaaaaaaaaalllllllllllll llllllllllllll!!!!!!!!!!!!!!!!!!!

What a strike! On his first professional start for Sociedad, Antoine had scored his first goal. He was off the mark! It was an incredible feeling, one that he would never, ever forget. He ran towards the corner flags, swinging his arms wildly. Antoine's cool goal celebrations would come a bit later. Instead, he just stood in front of the fans and kissed the club badge on his shirt.

'I knew you'd score today!' Agirretxe laughed as he gave Antoine a big hug. 'And that'll be the first of many, mate. Congratulations!'

CHAPTER 12

SOCIEDAD'S YOUNG STAR

What next for Sociedad's new Number 27? Well, Antoine kept starring – and his team kept winning! The doubters had disappeared; he was a fans' favourite already.

Against Salamanca, in October 2009, Xabi Prieto tapped a quick free kick to Dani Estrada, who crossed the ball into the six-yard box. Antoine made a striker's run ahead of Agirretxe and got there just in time. 1–0!

Gooooooooooooooooooooaaaaaaaaaaaaaaaalllllllllllll lllllllllllll!!!!!!!!!!!!!!!!!!!!!

'Come on!' Antoine yelled out as his happy teammates hugged him.

Despite being the new kid, he had already set himself a new challenge: leading Sociedad back into La Liga, the top division of Spanish football. Next season, Antoine wanted to be playing against Barcelona and Real Madrid, and their superstars Lionel Messi and Cristiano Ronaldo.

Only the top three teams in the Second Division would win promotion, however, and after two surprise defeats, Sociedad started to slip down the table. Would they have to wait another year?

'No way!' Antoine declared. He wasn't giving up yet, not until the very last kick of the season.

Against Recreativo de Huelva, Antoine raced down the left wing and skipped past a sliding tackle. As he dribbled into the penalty area, he looked up and crossed towards Agirretxe. But just as the striker looked certain to score, the goalkeeper stretched out an arm and pushed the ball away.

'Ohhhhhhhhhhhhhhhhhhhh!' groaned the Sociedad players and supporters in the Anoeta stadium.

Then just before half-time, Antoine curled a

brilliant free kick into the box, but Ion Ansotegi's header bounced back off the post.

'Ohhhhhhhhhhhhhhhhhhhhh!' they all groaned again.

With twenty minutes to go, Sociedad still hadn't scored. A draw wouldn't do; they had to win!

The rain was lashing down, but Antoine battled on. All he needed was one good goalscoring chance…

ZOOM! He raced past the Recreativo right-back and collected a pass on the edge of the area. This was it; he just had to stay calm. Antoine waited until the defenders were closing in, before shooting straight through the goalkeeper's legs. *Nutmeg!*

Goooooooooooooooooooaaaaaaaaaaaaaaaaalllllllllllll llllllllllll!!!!!!!!!!!!!!!!!!!!!

Eighteen-year-old Antoine had saved the day for Sociedad; he was the hero! Now, how should he celebrate his big moment? He jumped over the advertising boards, and then spotted an empty chair.

'A-ha – perfect!' Antoine thought to himself. He sat down in the chair and started clapping like he was a supporter in the crowd!

'You're crazy, kid,' his teammate Carlos Bueno called out, 'and we love you for that!'

Sociedad stayed in the Top Three for the rest of the season, with Antoine playing almost every minute of every match. Not only that, but he was also taking free kicks and corners like his hero, Becks. It was an amazing experience for such a young footballer. He had the support of his manager, his coaches, his teammates, *and* the fans. They were his second family and they gave him the confidence to show off his silky skills.

When a cross came in from the right wing, Antoine didn't bother taking a touch to control the ball; instead, he hit it first time with his right foot on the volley.

Goooooooooooooooooooooaaaaaaaaaaaaaaaaaalllllllllllll llllllllllllll!!!!!!!!!!!!!!!!!!!

Wow, what a superstrike! As he ran towards the corner flag, Antoine leapt high into the air.

His reputation was on the rise too. Word quickly spread about Sociedad's young star. Scouts came from all over Europe to see Antoine in action, and they liked what they saw. There was interest from Lyon, Arsenal, and even Becks's old club, Manchester United! Yes, Antoine was a wanted man, and Sociedad would have to act fast if they wanted to keep him.

They did. Soon, he was signing a big new five-year contract at the club. If one of the top teams really wanted to buy him, they would have to pay £30 million.

'Right, let's win the league now!' Antoine cheered happily.

With four games to go, Sociedad were top of the table with Levante, but only on goal difference. To claim the title, they had to keep winning and hope that Levante lost.

Sociedad beat Villarreal B, and Levante beat Rayo Vallecano. The two teams were tied on sixty-eight points!

'Hey, there's no need to panic,' Lasarte warned his players. 'Just play your normal way and we'll get those three points!'

Antoine was fully focused on achieving his target:

playing in La Liga. Away at Cadiz, he curled in another fantastic free kick and Carlos headed home. *GOAL!* Sociedad won 3–1 and their weekend got even better when Levante lost. They were now three points clear at the top. If they could just beat Celta Vigo, the Second Division title would be theirs!

The Anoeta Stadium was absolutely packed for the biggest game of the year. Everywhere that Antoine looked, he saw the colours of Sociedad.

Blue-and-white striped shirts,

blue-and-white striped scarves,

blue-and-white striped banners,

and even blue-and-white striped faces!

The supporters were nervous, but they still sang the club songs loudly and proudly.

'*Vamos, Real!*' they cheered.

What an atmosphere! If Sociedad won, it would be party time in the streets of San Sebastián. They couldn't let their fans down now...

Celta started well but Sociedad grew stronger as the game went on. Early in the second half, Carlos flicked the ball to Antoine, and he dribbled forward at top speed.

'Go on! Go on!' the fans urged him on.

This was it; his chance to win the title for his team. But as Antoine entered the penalty area, a defender came across and tripped him.

'Penalty!' he cried out as he lay there, sprawled across the grass.

When the referee pointed to the spot, the stadium went wild.

'We're going to win the league!' the fans shouted excitedly.

Xabi stepped up and... *GOAL – 1–0!*

Sociedad were so close now. Could they hold on to their lead?

Ten minutes later, Antoine battled bravely for a header at the back post. Too small to be a star? No way! He jumped the highest and headed it down for Carlos to score. *2–0!*

What a way for Antoine to end his incredible debut season! Six goals, lots of amazing assists, and now the Spanish Second Division title. It was beyond his wildest childhood dreams.

As soon as the final whistle went, the Sociedad players got the party started. Antoine, of course, was at the centre of all the fun. One minute, he was diving across the grass again and the next, he was dancing on Franck Songo'o's shoulders. He felt like Superman. It was easily the best night of his life so far.

Campeones, Campeones, Olé! Olé! Olé!

Unfortunately, Antoine didn't have very long to enjoy the moment. There would be no summer holiday for him that year, no well-deserved break. Instead, a few weeks after winning the league in Spain, he was heading home to France for the Under-19 European Championship.

CHAPTER 13

FRANCE'S YOUNG STAR

Yes, after his successful season in Spain, Antoine had attracted France's attention. It turned out that his country hadn't forgotten him, after all.

'Wow, thanks!' he told the Under-19s coach, Francis Smerecki, when he got the great news about his first international call-up.

Although Antoine didn't live in France any more, his family did, and he still felt French. Mâcon was his home and it always would be, no matter where he played his club football. Therefore, it was a huge honour for him to represent his country.

Antoine couldn't wait to wear the famous blue shirt. In only his second match for the Under-19s, he scored the winning goal against Ukraine. Smerecki had seen enough; he named Antoine in his squad for the UEFA 2010 Under-19 European Championship.

'I don't mind giving up my summer holiday for that!' Antoine joked with his brother, Theo.

Along with Spain, France were the favourites to win the whole tournament. They had home advantage and an excellent squad too. Their attack included Chelsea's wonderkid Gaël Kakuta, Lyon's Alexandre Lacazette, and now Antoine as well.

When the France senior team were knocked out in the first round of the 2010 World Cup, there was even more pressure on the Under-19s to perform well.

'Come on, let's lift that trophy!' Smerecki urged his players. France had lost in the semi-finals in both 2007 and 2009. This time, they were good enough to go all the way.

But what part would Antoine get to play? He was the new kid in the squad, and the others nicknamed him 'The Spaniard'. It wasn't a nasty nickname, but it did make him feel like the odd one out. Most of his teammates played for French clubs, and they had been playing together for years. Lots of them had been part of the France Under-17s team that lost to Spain in the Euro final two years earlier.

Oh well – Antoine would just have to work and work until he forced his way into the team. He was good at that!

France got off to a very strong start. In their first match, they thrashed the Netherlands 4–1. Antoine didn't manage to score, but he did in the second match against Austria. He grabbed two goals and so did Alexandre, in a 5–0 win.

'We're just too hot to handle!' they joked as they celebrated together.

Antoine was having the time of his life. The small, skinny boy from Mâcon was well on his way to becoming a superstar.

'"Griezmann" – remember the name!' his dad told people proudly.

France were on fire – could anyone stop them? Croatia did their best to beat them. They took the lead in the semi-final, but it didn't last long. Gaël got the equaliser and then Cédric Bakambu scored a late winner.

'Yes, you legend – we're in the final!' Antoine cheered as he chased after France's hero.

Their opponents in the final would be Spain, Antoine's second country. He had seen lots of their players in action and he knew how dangerous they could be. Thiago Alcântara was a midfield magician and Rodrigo could score from any angle. It was definitely going to be France's toughest test yet.

'We've got nothing to fear tonight,' Smerecki told the players before the big kick-off in Caen. 'Just go out there and make your country proud!'

Antoine was determined to become a national hero. As soon as the match started, he buzzed around the pitch, calling for the ball.

'Over here – pass it!'

Unfortunately, Antoine hardly had a touch because Spain were on top. They scored first and they nearly got a second.

'Keep going, we'll turn things around!' Antoine tried to encourage his teammates.

But France needed to get a goal quickly before it was too late. They had the home crowd behind them, but they were losing the battle out on the pitch.

'What's wrong?' Smerecki asked Antoine at half-time. He could see that his left winger was wincing with pain.

'It's nothing. My ankle hurts a bit, but I'll be fine to carry on!'

Antoine desperately wanted to keep playing, but instead, his manager decided to make a bold substitution. On came Yannis Tafer, and off went Antoine.

It was disappointing news, but Antoine didn't storm off in a sulk. No, he was too much of a team player to do that. If he couldn't help France out on the field, then he would try to help them from the bench instead.

'Come on, we can still win this!'

'Allez Les Bleus!'

When Yannis set up Gilles Sunu to make it 1–1, Antoine jumped up out of his seat just like all the other France supporters. He punched the air passionately. France were back in the game!

It was a fascinating final between two very talented teams, but there could only be one winner...

FRANCE! When his friend Alexandre headed in the winning goal, Antoine hobbled down the touchline to join in the big squad hug.

'Congratulations, I knew we could do it!' he shouted gleefully.

The France Under-19s were the Champions of Europe! Winning was a team effort and each of the players had played their part in the glorious success. Antoine hadn't been their hero in the final, but he had played well enough to make the Team of the Tournament, alongside Gaël and Cédric.

With a winners' medal around his neck and the glistening trophy in his hands, Antoine felt on top of the world. Could his life get any better? It could! The Under-19 Euros was only the start of Antoine's international adventures with France.

CHAPTER 14

LIGHTING UP
LA LIGA

When he returned to Spain after his Euro success,
Antoine had some catching up to do. Real Sociedad
told him to take two weeks off, but after only a
few days, he was desperate to get back out on the
football pitch.

'Can I come back early?' Antoine asked Lasarte.
'Please, I'm so bored!'

Plus, he didn't want to miss any more of the pre-
season training. What if someone else had caught
the manager's eye while he was away? Sociedad
were playing in La Liga now, against top teams like
Barcelona and Real Madrid. So, maybe Lasarte would
choose a more experienced winger...

'I'm back!' Antoine wanted to shout from the rooftops. 'Remember me?'

There were several new faces at the club. Sociedad had signed two new strikers, two new attacking midfielders... and a new left-winger. *Uh-oh!* Antoine would be competing with Francisco Sutil for one starting spot.

'Don't worry – if you play like you did last season,' Lasarte reassured him, 'you'll keep your place, no problem!'

Competition was good; it always brought out the best in Antoine. With his manager's support and his favourite Number 7 shirt, he was ready to spring into action. He would make his full La Liga debut against... Real Madrid!

'No big deal,' Antoine tried to tell himself, but it *was* a big deal. This was the moment he'd been dreaming about ever since he first joined Sociedad as a skinny little boy. This was the opportunity that he'd been waiting for, to test himself against Ronaldo and co.

In the first half, Sociedad's two big chances both

fell to Antoine. First, he snuck past the daydreaming Sergio Ramos to reach Xabi's cross.

'Here we go!' the Sociedad fans cheered, rising to their feet in excitement.

It was a free header in front of goal, and if he scored it, Antoine would be a club hero forever. Unfortunately, he didn't. He put way too much power on the header and the ball flew high over the crossbar.

'No! What a waste!' he screamed, swatting the air angrily.

A few minutes later, Raúl Tamudo played a great through-ball and Antoine sprinted past Ramos again.

'Here we go!' The Sociedad fans were back up on their feet. This time, they were even more excited because the ball was at Antoine's feet, rather than on his head. What could go wrong?

Antoine took one touch to control it and then *BANG!* But instead of trusting his right foot, he struck it awkwardly with the outside of his left foot. The shot whizzed just wide of the post.

'Not again!' he screamed in disbelief. He stood

there frozen with his hands on his head, and so did his teammates.

Oh dear, would his manager be angry with him? No – at half-time, Lasarte was full of encouragement. 'Keep going, you're causing them all kinds of problems!' he told Antoine.

It was Real Madrid who scored first, but Sociedad equalised straight away, and that was all thanks to Antoine, their danger man. He set up Raúl with a fantastic, fizzing free kick. *1–1!*

'Come on!' Antoine roared with a mix of joy and relief.

In the end, Ronaldo won the game with a free kick of his own, but Antoine didn't let that get him down. He was holding his own at the highest level. He was competing with the best players in the world now.

Antoine had his first La Liga assist, but what about his first La Liga goal? As each game passed, he grew more and more desperate to score, but that didn't help at all. He was hurrying shots and trying too hard.

'Just don't think about it,' Raúl replied when Antoine asked him for advice. 'You're playing well and that's what matters!'

When Antoine did finally get his first La Liga goal against Deportivo de La Coruña, it wasn't a very special strike. His celebration, however, was very special indeed. He jumped over the advertising boards at the Anoeta, and then spotted an empty car parked behind the goal.

'A-ha – perfect!' he thought to himself.

'Follow me!' he called to his teammates.

Antoine climbed into the front seat and started turning the steering wheel like he was driving the car! His teammates soon filled up the passenger seats.

'Grizi, you're crazy,' Xabi called out, 'and we love you for that!'

Now, that he was off the mark, Antoine could carry on lighting up La Liga. His manager kept his promise, and Antoine kept his place in the Sociedad team. Francisco who? Lasarte knew who his best left winger was.

Antoine scored in important victories over Málaga

and Getafe, and he set up goals against Sevilla and Atlético Madrid. What a superstar!

He knew that his main job was keeping Sociedad safe, but he liked to entertain as well whenever he could. For him, football was about winning *and* having fun. When he scored his second goal against Sporting Gijón, he celebrated by standing with one of the stadium stewards.

'I love this club!' Antoine said, looking up at all the singing, dancing fans.

At the age of nineteen, he was learning how to be the best by playing against the best. La Liga was the greatest football education ever!

Messi's Barcelona battered Sociedad 5–0 at the Nou Camp, but it was a different story at home at the Anoeta. Antoine and his teammates fought back from 1–0 down to beat the league leaders 2–1.

'We did it!' the players cried happily as they hugged each other. 'We're staying up!'

It was a historic win that saved Sociedad from being relegated back to the Second Division.

In the second match of the 2011–12 season,

however, the stars of Barcelona returned to the Anoeta, eager for revenge.

Alexis Sánchez passed to Xavi. *1–0!*

Xavi passed to Cesc Fàbregas. *2–0!*

Was it game over already, after only twelve minutes? The Sociedad supporters feared the worst, but down on the pitch, their players persevered.

Xabi crossed to Agirretxe. *2–1!*

'Yes, we can do this!' Antoine shouted, throwing his arms up in the air.

Agirretxe's next shot hit the crossbar but Antoine raced in to score the rebound. 2–2!

Gooooooooooooooooooooaaaaaaaaaaaaaaaaalllllllllllll llllllllllllllll!!!!!!!!!!!!!!!!!!!

What a comeback! Even when Messi came on, Sociedad stayed strong.

At the final whistle, Antoine punched the air with passion. This was where he belonged now – at La Liga's highest level, battling it out with Messi and Ronaldo.

CHAPTER 15

INTERNATIONAL UPS
AND DOWNS

France's Under-19 Euro winners were soon off on
another big international adventure: to the FIFA
Under-20 World Cup in Colombia.

Yippeeeeeee!

Antoine was full of excitement as the squad
set off for South America. He couldn't wait to get
started. The Under-20 World Cup was a very special
tournament with so much history. Diego Maradona
had been the star player back in 1979, then Messi
in 2005, and Sergio Agüero in 2007. Could it be
Antoine's turn in 2011? Hopefully! He was ready to
shine with the eyes of the world watching him.

France's first match was against Colombia,

the hosts. Their coach warned them about the
atmosphere before kick-off.

'It's going to be really loud out there tonight,'
Smerecki said. 'So, try your best to ignore the boos
and get on with the game, okay?'

'Yes, Coach!'

When Gilles scored, France looked like they would
cruise to a comfortable victory. But instead, they
were destroyed by Colombia's deadly duo, James
Rodríguez and Luis Muriel. Out on the left-wing,
Antoine couldn't believe what he was seeing. The
goals just kept going in.

1–1, 2–1, 3–1, 4–1 to Colombia!

It was a really embarrassing result for France, but
their World Cup wasn't over yet. If they won their
next two matches, they would still go through.

France 3–1 South Korea,

France 2–0 Mali.

Job done! They were in the second round, but that
didn't satisfy Antoine. So far, he didn't have a single
goal or assist in the tournament. He was playing his
worst football in ages.

'You guys play better when I'm not on the pitch,' he argued grumpily.

'Rubbish!' Gaël replied. 'We need you, Grizi. You'll get a goal soon!'

Antoine nearly scored in the first half against Ecuador. His free kick curled high over the wall and only just wide of the post.

'Nearly!' he groaned.

The minutes ticked by and still France couldn't score a winning goal. Antoine set up glorious chances for Clément Grenier and Cédric but they both missed the target.

It was no good; Antoine would have to score the winner himself, and he didn't have long left to do it. In fact, if he didn't do something special soon, Smerecki would take him off. Gaël and Alexandre were on the bench, watching and waiting.

'It's now or never,' Antoine muttered to himself.

As he chased after another hopeful long ball, the Ecuador defenders called, 'OFFSIDE!' but the linesperson's flag stayed down.

Antoine was through on goal, one on one with the

keeper to win the match for France! His first shot was saved but not his second.

Goooooooooooooooooooaaaaaaaaaaaaaaaaallllllllllll llllllllllllll!!!!!!!!!!!!!!!!!!!!!

Antoine had done it; at last, he was a World Cup hero! He ran over to celebrate with the substitutes behind the goal. Winning was a team effort, after all.

At the final whistle, the France players hugged and high-fived. Thanks to Antoine, they were through to the quarter-finals. And after 120 tense minutes of football against Nigeria, they were through to the semi-finals! Portugal were now the last team standing between France and the Under-20 World Cup Final.

'Come on, we're so close!' Smerecki urged his players on.

But unfortunately, France conceded two goals in the first half and this time, they couldn't fight back. Despite Antoine's best efforts, his World Cup dream was over... for now.

'Never mind, in a few years, we'll be playing in the senior tournament,' Alexandre declared confidently as they clapped the French fans in the stadium. 'World Cup 2014 – see you there, bro!'

Antoine nodded and managed a small smile. It was disappointing, but he did feel like he was on the path to international glory. From the Under-20s, he soon moved up to the Under-21s and from there, it would only be one short step to the senior squad.

'It's only a matter of time,' his proud brother, Theo, assured him.

That last short step, however, turned out to be a giant leap. It would be nearly three long years before Antoine made his senior debut for France.

It was all because of one silly mistake. In October 2012, the France Under-21s faced Norway in the play-offs to qualify for Euro 2013. When they won the home leg 1–0, the young players were in the mood to celebrate.

'Hey, we're only halfway there,' their manager, Erick Mombaerts, warned them. 'We've still got to win the second leg in Norway next week.'

Unfortunately, some members of the squad didn't listen. Five young players decided to sneak out of the team hotel to go partying, and Antoine was one of them. When Mombaerts found out the next day, he was furious.

'You're meant to be professional footballers!' the Under-21 manager shouted. 'We've got a game in three days and we need to prepare, not party. You've really let yourselves and your country down.'

That second leg turned out to be a total disaster for France. With twenty minutes to go, Norway were winning 5–1! Antoine came on and scored, but it was too little too late. France wouldn't be playing at Euro 2013 after all.

Antoine felt very embarrassed and ashamed of himself. He had made a silly mistake, and he had paid the price for it. It was an important lesson for a young player to learn.

'I'm sorry, it won't happen again!' he promised Mombaerts.

A month later, however, Antoine was banned from the French national teams for a whole year. During that time, he couldn't play for the Under-21s *or* the seniors.

'No way, that's not fair!' Antoine protested at first, but it was no use. He had to accept his punishment and just wait for it to end.

'You know you could always play for Portugal instead...' Theo suggested one day during that difficult year.

Yes, thanks to their Grandad Amaro, that was still a possibility for Antoine. He did think about it briefly, but not for very long. He was born in France and he felt 100 per cent French. Plus, he was determined to follow in the footsteps of his idols, the heroes of 1998: Barthez, Lizarazu, Henry and, best of all, Zidane.

Yes, Antoine would just have to wait for his turn to be a French hero.

CHAPTER 16

SOCIEDAD'S SHINING STAR

While he waited to make his international comeback, Antoine carried on shining for his club, Real Sociedad. The fans loved their little French magician, or 'The Little Devil' as they now called him. Each season, Antoine got better and better. After scoring seven goals in his first year, he then scored eight in the next, and then eleven in the year after that.

During the 2012–13 season, Antoine helped take Sociedad from mid-table all the way up into the La Liga Top Six. No, they weren't on the same level as Barcelona and Real Madrid yet, but they did have a fantastic front four: Agirretxe up front, with Xabi just behind, then Carlos Vela on the right and, of course, Antoine on the left.

'There's no stopping us now!'

Not only was he getting more goals, but Antoine was also getting more important goals. He scored in both of Sociedad's local derby wins against Athletic Bilbao, and in a thrilling draw with Real Madrid. This time, when the cross came to him at the back post, Antoine didn't waste his chance.

Gooooooooooooooooooooaaaaaaaaaaaaaaaalllllllllllll lllllllllllllll!!!!!!!!!!!!!!!!!!!!

'Come on!' Antoine roared as he leapt up, swinging his fist at the sky.

With one game to go, Sociedad were in fifth place, two points behind Valencia. If they finished fifth, they would qualify for the Europa League. But if they finished fourth, they would qualify for the greatest club competition on earth, the Champions League.

'We *have* to win this!' Antoine told his teammates before their final match against Deportivo de La Coruña.

Playing in the Champions League had been

Antoine's childhood dream. As a young boy in Mâcon, he had watched Nedvěd, Zidane and Beckham all starring on football's biggest stage. Was he about to get his chance at last? Sociedad were so close, and Valencia had a tough trip to Sevilla. Anything could happen...

But first things first: Sociedad had to win at Deportivo.

Carlos dribbled through the defence and took a shot, but the keeper made a comfortable save.

'Unlucky!' Antoine clapped to encourage his teammate.

After twenty minutes, Sociedad's star wingers swapped places. On the left, Carlos collected the ball and passed it through to Agirretxe.

'Over here!' Antoine called out, waving his arms in the air. He was in so much space on the right.

Agirretxe decided to strike it himself, but the rebound fell right at Antoine's feet. This was it – his chance to be the hero who shot Sociedad into the Champions League! As the goalkeeper rushed across his line, Antoine coolly aimed for the opposite corner.

The ball clipped the post on its way into the net.

Gooooooooooooooooooooaaaaaaaaaaaaaaaaaalllllllllllll llllllllllllll!!!!!!!!!!!!!!!!!!!!!

There was no cool celebration – not yet. Antoine was saving that for when they won the match and qualified for the Champions League. At half-time, it was all looking good. Sociedad were 1–0 up and Valencia were 2–1 down.

'Just stay focused on our own match!' Sociedad's manager Philippe Montanier urged.

Sociedad didn't score a second goal, but they held on to their lead. Valencia, meanwhile, had lost 4–3 to Sevilla...

As the referee blew the final whistle, Antoine booted the ball high into the stands. 'We did it!' he cheered, throwing his arms up triumphantly.

Agirretxe was the first to run over and give him a big hug. 'You're a club legend now!' he cried out.

Thanks to Antoine's goal, Sociedad had finished in fourth place in La Liga. Next season, they would be playing in the Champions League!

They wouldn't go straight into the group stage,

however. First, they would have to win a play-off against...

...Lyon! The team that Antoine had supported as a boy, and the team that had decided that he was too small to be a star! He couldn't wait to show them what a mistake they had made.

For the first leg, Antoine travelled back home to France and back to the Stade de Gerland where his dad had taken him to see his first ever football match.

'Good luck!' he said to his friend from the France Under-20s, Alexandre. They would be playing on opposite teams.

'Yeah, may the best team win!' replied Alexandre.

Antoine was going to make sure that was Real Sociedad. He had even dyed his hair bright blond for the big occasion.

Early in the first half, Carlos chased down the left wing and looked up for the cross. Was there anyone there? Yes, Antoine was racing into the penalty area...

The ball was behind him, but in a flash, Antoine

swivelled his body and went for the spectacular. He jumped up and swung his left foot forward. *BANG!* His technique was perfect and so was his power and direction. The ball flew into the bottom corner before the goalkeeper had even moved.

Goooooooooooooooooooaaaaaaaaaaaaaaaaallllllllllll llllllllllllll!!!!!!!!!!!!!!!!!!!

On his return to Lyon, Antoine had just scored his best goal ever! With the adrenaline rushing through him, he felt like a superstar – no, a super*hero*. He ran over and jumped into Carlos's arms.

'Yes, yes, YES!'

In the second half, Haris Seferović scored another wondergoal for Sociedad.

'That was almost as good as mine!' Antoine joked as they celebrated together.

It finished 2–0 in France, and eight days later, it finished 2–0 in Spain. At home at the Anoeta, Antoine didn't score but he did set one up for Carlos. Sociedad were through to the Champions League group stage!

Their opponents would be Shakhtar Donetsk,

Bayer Leverkusen, and Becks's old club, Manchester United.

'Bring it on!' Antoine said with a cheeky smile. 'The Little Devil' was ready to give Europe's top defenders a trip to hell and back.

Unfortunately, it didn't work out that way. No, Antoine didn't enjoy his first Champions League experience at all. Sociedad lost five of their six games, and they only scored one goal – a penalty taken by Carlos.

Against Manchester United, Antoine hit a fierce, curling free kick but it struck the post. *So close!*

'Oh well, there's always next time,' he told himself as he trudged off the Old Trafford pitch after a 1–0 defeat.

There was no way that he was going to let that be his one and only Champions League adventure.

CHAPTER 17

WORLD CUP 2014

At the start of 2014, the ban on Antoine playing for France was finally lifted. Hurray – his silly mistake was behind him at last! He now had six months to force his way into the senior squad before the start of the 2014 World Cup in Brazil.

'Easy!' he declared confidently.

The problem was that France's first international match of the year wasn't until March. Oh well, he would just have to keep shining for Real Sociedad and hope that the national manager was watching.

Fortunately, Didier Deschamps was watching Antoine closely:

He saw his thundering strike against Athletic

Bilbao, his cheeky lob and powerful header against Elche, and his marvellous performance against Messi's Barcelona too.

With the score at 1–1, Carlos crossed to Antoine, who slid in to chip the ball over Víctor Valdés.

Goooooooooooooooooooaaaaaaaaaaaaaaaaalllllllllllll llllllllllllll!!!!!!!!!!!!!!!!!!!!

Five minutes later, Antoine set up Sociedad's third goal with a clever pass to David Zurutuza.

Deschamps was very impressed. Antoine could play in all three attacking positions – right wing, left wing, or even striker! That made him a very useful addition indeed. When the manager picked his squad for France's match against the Netherlands, there was a new name next to Franck Ribéry, Olivier Giroud and Karim Benzema:

'A. Griezmann.'

'I'm in!' Antoine told his family straight away.

'Congratulations, we're so proud of you!' his parents cried.

'What did I tell you?' Theo laughed. 'It was only a matter of time!'

Antoine didn't merely make his international debut as a substitute; he played right from the start. With Franck out injured, the France front three was Karim in the middle, Mathieu Valbuena on the right, and Antoine on the left. What a moment! His whole family was there at the Stade de France for his big day.

'We love you, Antoine!' they cheered proudly.

Antoine felt emotional just walking out onto the pitch wearing his country's famous blue shirt. By the time the national anthem began, he was almost in tears.

'Not now,' he told himself, 'this is my time to shine!'

Mathieu crossed the ball to Antoine, who passed it first-time to Karim on the volley. His header was going in, but it was blocked on the goal line.

'Excellent!' Deschamps clapped on the sidelines.

France went on to beat the Netherlands 2–0. Antoine didn't get a debut goal or assist, but he was off to a strong start.

What next? Antoine was hungry for more international action, but he would have to wait another two months. By then, Deschamps had already named his squad for World Cup 2014 and... Antoine was in!

'Yes!' he cheered with his fists clenched. 'Brazil, here I come!'

Before that, however, France had three friendlies to play. If he wanted to be a World Cup hero, Antoine would need to do something special...

It didn't happen against Norway, but it did happen against Paraguay. With ten minutes to go, the ball came to Antoine on the edge of a crowded penalty area.

'Now's your chance!' he told himself. 'Don't waste it!'

Time seemed to stand still as Antoine controlled the pass and then curled a looping shot over every head and down into the bottom corner.

Goooooooooooooooooooaaaaaaaaaaaaaaaaallllllllllll llllllllllllll!!!!!!!!!!!!!!!!!!!

It was definitely special! Antoine chose his favourite celebration for his first international goal – an awesome knee-slide.

'*Allez Les Bleus!*' he roared like a lion.

In the final friendly against Jamaica, Antoine only came on with twenty minutes to go, but he still managed to score two goals. The second was even a cheeky backheel! But had he done enough to earn a World Cup starting spot? He would have to wait and see.

Antoine had played at the 2011 Under-20 World Cup in Colombia, but that was nothing compared to this. This was an international celebration of football in the best possible place – Brazil! Everywhere the players went, there was a real party atmosphere – the beaches, the stadiums *and* the streets.

'Right, time to focus on football!' Antoine told himself.

For France's first game against Honduras, Franck was out, and that meant Antoine was in. Wow, his World Cup dream was really coming true.

In the first-half, France hit the crossbar twice: first, Blaise Matuidi, and then Antoine with a header.

'Noooooo!' he groaned with his hands on his head. What a missed opportunity to score on his

World Cup debut! Instead, it was Karim who became France's hero.

In France's second group match, against Switzerland, Antoine was out, and Olivier was in. He watched from the bench as his teammates got goal after goal: Olivier, then Blaise, then Mathieu, then Karim, and then Moussa Sissoko. 5–0!

'What about me?' Antoine wondered. 'I want to join in!'

But when he finally came on, the game was already over. Were France better off without him? When Antoine started their final group game against Ecuador, they drew 0–0.

'Just relax, Grizi,' his teammate Paul Pogba told him. 'You're trying too hard!'

Antoine was usually a pretty chilled-out guy, but this was the World Cup they were talking about! The heroes of 1998 and 2002 had inspired him as a kid, and now he was following in their footsteps.

'I'll relax when we've won the trophy!' he replied.

Antoine was back on the bench for France's Round of 16 match against Nigeria. But with thirty minutes to go, it was still 0–0. Deschamps looked at his substitutes and gave Antoine the sign:

'Get ready – you're coming on!'

From the moment he ran on to the pitch, Antoine changed the game. He linked up brilliantly with Karim and Mathieu, playing quick passes and clever one-twos. Maybe France weren't better off without him, after all. They were getting closer and closer, but they still needed to score...

A corner-kick flew high over Antoine's head, but Paul was there at the back post. *1–0!*

'Finally!' the French players cried out with relief.

Could Antoine make it 2–0? He dribbled down the left wing and shot from the edge of the area, but the Nigeria keeper made an excellent save.

'Noooooo!' Antoine groaned with his hands on his head again. It hadn't been Antoine's lucky World Cup so far.

In the last minute, France doubled their lead, and Antoine played a key part. His run into the six-yard box made Joseph Yobo panic and he ended up scoring an own goal.

'I didn't touch the ball, but that's still MY goal!'
Antoine told Mathieu with a cheeky smile.

The goal was given to Yobo, but it had helped
Antoine to earn his starting spot back for the quarter-
final against Germany. He was delighted when he
saw Deschamps's teamsheet. Just like in his France
debut three months earlier, it was Karim in the
middle, Mathieu Valbuena on the right, and Antoine
on the left.

'Let's win this!' their captain Hugo Lloris shouted,
clapping his goalkeeper gloves together.

But after thirteen minutes, France were 1–0
down. The nation was relying on their front three
to fight back...

Antoine crossed to Mathieu, who chested the
ball down and struck it fiercely towards the bottom
corner. Manuel Neuer dived down to make a super
save, but Karim looked certain to score the rebound.
Were France about to equalise? No, because Mats
Hummels jumped up bravely to block his shot.

'Keep going, the goal is coming!' Antoine urged his
teammates as he ran over to take the corner-kick.

He was full of belief but sadly, so was the German defence. France tried and tried but there was just no way past Neuer. At the final whistle, their tournament was over.

All the French players were devastated, but especially Antoine. He hated losing any football match, so losing a World Cup quarter-final hurt like hell. As his tears fell, he wiped them away with the bottom of his shirt.

'Hey, we did our best,' Paul comforted his friend. 'It didn't work out this time, but this is just the start for us, Grizi. We're going to come back bigger and stronger for Euro 2016. We'll be unstoppable!'

CHAPTER 18

NEW ADVENTURES AT ATLÉTICO

Antoine returned to Spain but this time, he didn't return to Real Sociedad. Instead, he was off on an exciting new adventure.

'I arrived here as a boy and I leave as a man,' he told the media in July 2014. 'I want to thank the staff, the supporters and the players for the last ten incredible years.'

Real Sociedad had always believed in Antoine, even when he had been a small, skinny thirteen-year-old boy. He would always be grateful for that, but he felt like he had fully repaid their faith. During his five seasons in the first team, the club had risen all the way from the Spanish Second Division to the Champions League. What a turnaround! Now, however, it was time for a new challenge.

'We'll miss you, Grizi!' the supporters cried out.

But where would Antoine go? After scoring twenty goals for Sociedad and then starring for France at the World Cup, suddenly he had so many options.

'How do you feel about returning to France?' his agent asked him. Monaco were looking for a new superstar to help them compete with PSG.

'Or maybe you'd prefer a move to England?' The top Premier League clubs were also queuing up to buy him: Manchester United, Arsenal, Tottenham, Chelsea...

Antoine shook his head. 'No, I want to stay in Spain for now.'

There was one La Liga club that was top of his list – Atlético Madrid. They had been trying to sign Antoine since 2011. Back then, they had wanted him to replace their star striker Sergio Agüero, who had just signed for Manchester City. That summer, Real Sociedad refused to sell Antoine, but Atlético didn't give up on him. Three years later, they returned with a much bigger offer: £24 million. It was an offer the club had to accept.

'Right, let's do the deal!' Antoine told his agent.

Atlético felt like the perfect place for him to grow as a player. Under Diego Simeone, their amazing Argentinian manager, the club had just beaten Barcelona and Real Madrid to the Spanish League title, and they had reached the Champions League Final too.

'That's my dream!' Antoine exclaimed excitedly.

The team had a deadly defence and a hard-working midfield, but Atlético had just lost their two top goalscorers – Diego Costa and David Villa. Who would replace them? Simeone had already signed the Croatian striker Mario Mandžukić but he also wanted an attacker with speed and skill, who could create chances *and* score goals.

The Atlético manager had made up his mind; that attacker was Antoine. He was a big game player and he had proved it with that acrobatic volley against Lyon and that cool chip against Barcelona.

'You'll be our Messi!' Simeone declared confidently. 'Our Ronaldo!'

'Yes please!' Antoine replied. It was his ideal role. He didn't want to go to Barcelona and sit on the bench behind Messi, Neymar Jr and Luis Suárez. Antoine was twenty-three years old now and ready to take on the responsibility of being a team leader.

From the moment he arrived in Madrid, Antoine was treated like a star. He was Atlético's big signing of the summer, after all. Simeone greeted him with a smile and a firm handshake.

'It's great to have you here. I hope you're ready to win lots of trophies!'

'You bet, boss!'

TV cameras followed Antoine everywhere, even into the medical room. As he lay back in the doctor's chair, he gave a big thumbs-up.

'I'm very excited and happy to join the Atleti family,' he said in his first interview for the club website.

Antoine couldn't wait to start playing football, but

first, their super signing had to be introduced to
the supporters.

'Griezmann! Griezmann! Griezmann!' chanted
6,000 fans as Antoine walked out onto the pitch at
the Vicente Calderón Stadium, wearing the full club
kit. When he raised his arms up to wave, the noise
got even louder. It was an unbelievable feeling.

'This must be what it's like to be Messi!' he
thought to himself.

With his hair slicked back and Number Seven on
the back of his red-and-white-striped shirt, Antoine
looked as stylish as his hero, David Beckham. But did
he have the skills to go with that style?

Of course! After posing for lots of photos, Antoine
entertained the Atleti fans with some keepy-uppies.
Pressure, what pressure? It was like he was back
at the basketball court in Mâcon. With everyone
watching, he went through his full routine:

*Right foot, left foot, right knee, left knee, chest,
head, right shoulder, left shoulder... SELFIE TIME!*

Antoine lifted his phone up high to get as many
people in the photo as possible. 'On the count of

three, everyone say "Atleti". Three, two, one...'

ATLETI!!

The fans loved their new superstar already, but Antoine would still need to prove himself on the pitch. What better way to do that than by helping them to beat their Madrid rivals, Real, in the Spanish Super Cup?

Before that, however, Antoine had lots of work to do on the training field. At Atlético, everyone was expected to chase back and defend, even the attackers. So, Simeone made sure that all his players were super-fit. His sessions were a lot more intense and tiring than the ones at Real Sociedad, but Antoine was a fast learner when it came to football. He listened carefully to his manager's instructions and tried his best to impress him.

'Right, it's time for revenge!' Simeone urged his team before kick-off at the Bernabeu. Real had beaten them in the 2014 Champions League Final and the players wanted payback.

When Antoine came off the bench in the second-half, the score was still 0–0. 'Great!' he thought to himself as he ran into position. 'I can become a club hero straight away!'

Sadly, Antoine couldn't create any super-sub chances, but Simeone put him in the Atleti starting line-up for the second leg back at the Vicente Calderón.

'We're gonna win tonight,' he told his strike partner, Mario. 'I can feel it!'

In the second minute of the match, Antoine jumped for a header against Sergio Ramos and managed to flick the ball cleverly through to Mario. He fired a fierce shot into Iker Casillas's bottom corner. *GOAL! 1–0 to Atlético!*

Antoine was delighted with his first assist for his new club. He chased after Mario, pumping his fists at the crowd. 'I told you!' he screamed in his strike partner's ear.

For the next ninety minutes, the players worked really hard to protect their lead. At the final whistle, the Spanish Super Cup was theirs! Antoine had already won his first trophy with Atlético.

'The first of many!' he cheered happily with his new teammates.

CHAPTER 19

THE CHAMPIONS LEAGUE CHALLENGE

Atlético were playing the Greek team Olympiakos in the Champions League. Koke passed to Juanfran and then ran down the right wing, calling for the return pass. As he looked up, he could see Antoine over on the left wing, pointing at the six-yard box. He was about to make his striker's sprint.

'Play it now!' he shouted.

The cross was perfect, and so was Antoine's cool side-foot finish.

Gooooooooooooooooooooaaaaaaaaaaaaaaaalllllllllllll llllllllllllll!!!!!!!!!!!!!!!!!!!

It was Antoine's first goal for Atlético and his first in the Champions League too. However, there was no time for a special celebration. His team was losing 3–2 to Olympiakos.

'Cheers, mate!' Antoine said, bumping fists with Koke as they raced back for the restart.

Despite that early defeat, Atlético still finished top of their group, ahead of Olympiakos and Juventus. Next up: Bayer Leverkusen in the Round of 16.

'We're good enough to thrash them!' Antoine declared confidently.

On top of his two Champions League strikes, he had also scored fourteen times in La Liga, including a hat-trick against Athletic Bilbao. Antoine was on fire! Simeone didn't see him as a tricky winger anymore; he saw him as a star striker with clever movement and a lethal left foot. Antoine was improving all the time in his new role, and he was hungry for more goals and more glory.

'Well if we don't thrash them, that new hairstyle of yours is going to look really stupid!' Koke teased him.

Unfortunately, Atlético lost 1–0 in Germany, and could only win 1–0 back in Madrid. With the scores tied, it was time for penalties!

'I want to take one,' Antoine told Simeone straight away. His team needed him, and he wasn't going to let them down.

Raúl García missed Atleti's first spot kick, which meant that Antoine really had to score. Pressure, what pressure? After a short run-up, he slammed his shot into the top corner of the net.

'Grizi! Grizi! Grizi!' the fans chanted as he jogged back to the halfway line to join his teammates. Job done!

After Antoine's cool strike, Atlético went on to win the shoot-out. They were through to the Champions League quarter-finals, where they would face... Real Madrid!

'No way, not again!' Koke complained.

'Hey, it's fine,' Antoine argued. 'We beat them in the Super Cup, and we thrashed them 4–0 in La Liga last month. We can do this!'

Why should Atlético be scared of anyone? To win the Champions League, they would have to beat the best teams in Europe. Antoine relished the challenge.

It finished 0–0 in the first leg at the Vicente Calderón, and it was still 0–0 with five minutes to go in the second leg at the Bernabéu. Were Atlético heading for another penalty shoot-out? No, Cristiano dribbled through their defence and set up Javier Hernández to score. *1–0 to Real Madrid!*

'Noooooo!' Antoine groaned on the Atleti bench. He had already been subbed off, so there was nothing more that he could do to help his team. Their 2015 Champions League challenge was over, and soon, so was their La Liga title challenge.

'Next year,' Simeone promised his disappointed players. 'We'll be back, and stronger than ever!'

Until then, Antoine would have to settle for being Atlético's top scorer, and one of the best attackers in Spain. At the La Liga Awards, the 'Team of the Season' featured a front three of:

Ronaldo,

Messi,

and… Antoine!

'Congratulations,' his teammates cheered. 'You're

a real superstar now!'

In that moment, Antoine knew that he had made the right choice by joining Atlético. With the support of his amazing manager and teammates, he was getting better and better. And now, after a strong first season, it was time for him to take the next step, and lead his team to Champions League glory...

Antoine scored four goals in six games, as Atlético finished top of their group again. And again, they won on penalties in the Round of 16. This time, Antoine took his team's first spot kick and sent the PSV goalkeeper the wrong way.

'Grizi! Grizi! Grizi!' the fans chanted as he jogged back to the halfway line to join his teammates. Job done! Atlético were through to the Champions League quarter-finals, where they would face... Barcelona.

'Why do we always get the toughest draws?' Koke complained.

'Hey, it's fine,' Antoine argued. 'You guys beat them in the quarters back in 2014. That was before I arrived, and now we're even better!'

Atlético lost the first leg away at the Nou Camp, but at least Fernando Torres had scored an away goal. That gave them hope for victory back at the Vicente Calderón.

As he waited for kick-off, Antoine took a deep breath and focused on the game ahead. Atleti had to make the most of their home advantage. Up in the stands, their fans never stopped singing, and that noise would spur them on to a special win.

'Come on!' he clapped.

Fernando was suspended, so Antoine was Atlético's main striker. He was always on the move, looking to escape from the Barcelona centre-backs.

'Play it now!'

As the cross came in from the left, Antoine was in lots of space near the edge of the penalty area. He got his head to the ball, but the goalkeeper made a comfortable save.

'Too easy! That needed much more power.'

Antoine was annoyed at himself, but his manager was full of encouragement. 'Great run, Grizi – keep going!'

From the right wing, Saúl curled another dangerous cross into the box. Antoine was in a perfect position between the Barcelona defenders. He leapt into the air and headed the ball much more powerfully this time.

Goooooooooooooooooooaaaaaaaaaaaaaaaaalllllllllllll llllllllllllll!!!!!!!!!!!!!!!!!!!!

Antoine was so excited that he thought his chest might explode. It was easily one of the most important goals that he had ever scored.

'Yes!' Saúl screamed, throwing his arms around Antoine.

'You hero!' Koke cried out after they had done their cool handshake celebration together.

Would Barcelona bounce back? The trio of Messi, Suárez and Neymar (MSN) attacked again and again, but the Atlético defence was so strong. In the end, it was Antoine who scored the only other goal of the game. He stepped up to the spot and squeezed his penalty into the bottom corner.

Goooooooooooooooooooaaaaaaaaaaaaaaaaalllllllllllll

///////////////////!!!!!!!!!!!!!!!!!!!!!!

2–0 to Atlético! Thanks to Antoine, they were
going through to the Champions League semi-finals.
At the final whistle, the players bounced up and
down together in front of the fans. What a night!
The smile stayed on Antoine's face for days. Atleti
were now just two games away from the final.
All they had to do was beat Pep Guardiola's Bayern
Munich.

'Hey, we're good enough to beat anyone!' Antoine
declared confidently.

Saúl's wonder goal was enough to win the home
leg, but out in Germany, Bayern were almost
unbeatable. Even when they scored first, however,
Atlético never gave up. All they needed was one
away goal...

Early in the second half, Antoine nodded the
ball down to Fernando and then ZOOM! He
sprinted past the Bayern defenders to collect the
one-two. What a chance! He was one-on-one with
their sweeper keeper, Manuel Neuer. If he scored,
Atlético would be forty minutes away from a place

in the Champions League final. If he missed, the fans would hate him forever.

Pressure, what pressure? Antoine kept his cool and picked his spot perfectly.

Goooooooooooooooooooooaaaaaaaaaaaaaaaaaallllllllllllll llllllllllllllll!!!!!!!!!!!!!!!!!!

He had done it; he was Atlético's hero and he had led his team all the way back to the Champions League final. Antoine stood in front of the fans and started his new 'Hotline Bling' celebration. But before he could finish, his teammates lifted him high into the air.

'Yes, Grizi!'

'What a hero!'

Antoine couldn't wait for the main event to begin. The 2016 Champions League Final would be a repeat of 2014 – Atlético Madrid vs Real Madrid. Atleti had lost that time, but since then, they had signed a world-class superstar: Antoine. His goals had helped them beat Messi's Barcelona, so why not Ronaldo's Real too?

As he walked out onto the San Siro pitch, Antoine

looked as cool as ever. He strolled straight past the glistening trophy and smiled at each of his opponents as he shook their hands. Why shouldn't he be happy? Antoine was playing in his first important final. He was just one more win away from lifting the Champions League trophy.

'Enjoy it, this is your time to shine!' That's what everyone had told him.

Unfortunately, the first goal of the final went to Real, and it was Sergio Ramos who scored it.

'Not again!' the Atleti players thought, but they didn't give up. That wasn't the team's style at all. Instead, they picked themselves up and played on. There was still plenty of time to score.

Antoine, however, was acting like a superstar in a hurry. He took shot after shot from every possible angle. Some flew over, some trickled wide, and some were saved by the goalkeeper – but not one of them went in.

'Take your time!' Simeone urged at half-time.

Things soon looked brighter in the second half. When Antoine passed the ball forward, Pepe lunged in and fouled Fernando.

'Penalty!' Antoine cried out.

The referee pointed to the spot straight away. What a chance for Antoine and Atlético! He placed the ball down and then took a few steps back.

'It's no big deal,' he told himself. 'It's no different to taking a penalty in training!'

But Antoine couldn't help getting overexcited. His strike was a little too hard and a little too high. The ball crashed back off the crossbar and bounced away.

PENALTY MISSED!

Antoine felt sick with guilt. He had let the club down at the crucial moment. However, there was no time to dwell on that mistake. He would have nightmares about that penalty for weeks to come, but for now, Atleti were still in the game. And the only way to make it up to his teammates was to keep creating chances...

With ten minutes to go, Yannick Carrasco slid in to score at the back post. *1–1!* Antoine was so relieved that he raced over to thank his teammate.

'Yes, Yannick – you legend!'

In the end, the 2016 Champions League Final went all the way to penalties. Would Antoine be brave enough to take another one for Atlético after his earlier miss?

Of course he would! His team needed him, and he wasn't going to let them down again. Antoine went first and coolly sent the keeper the wrong way.

'Come on!' he roared. 'We can win this!'

But Atlético's hopes soon faded when Juanfran's penalty hit the post. Ronaldo stepped up and won it for Real.

What a cruel blow! It was a heartbreaking moment for Antoine and his teammates. They lay sprawled out on the grass in shocked silence. After 120 minutes of football and nine nail-biting penalty kicks, they were exhausted and defeated. What was there left to say? Atlético had lost in the Champions League Final... again.

Simeone talked to each of his players and tried his best to lift their spirits.

'Please don't blame yourself,' he told Antoine, putting a strong arm around his shoulder. 'We win as a team and we lose as a team. You've been brilliant all season, Grizi. You're now one of the best players in the world. I know it hurts but use that pain to lead us back here next year!'

CHAPTER 20

EURO 2016

In the meantime, could Antoine use his Champions League pain to lead France to glory? His country was counting on him. They were the hosts of Euro 2016, and at the previous international tournament held in France, Zidane and co. had won the 1998 World Cup.

'No pressure then!' Paul joked, trying to cheer Antoine up.

They were the leaders of the new-look French team. In attack, there was no Karim, no Mathieu and no Franck. Olivier would be the main striker, with Dimitri Payet on one wing and Antoine on the other, and Paul bursting forward from midfield.

For Antoine, expectations were higher than ever.
He had shown for Atlético that he was now one of
the best players in the world, up there with Messi
and Ronaldo. It was time to prove it for France
too, in front of huge home crowds: at the Stade de
France in Paris, the Stade Vélodrome in Marseille,
and maybe even Lyon's new Parc Olympique
Lyonnais, just fifty miles from Antoine's childhood
home in Mâcon.

'Grizi, we'll have to win our group if you want to
play there!' Paul said, looking at the fixture list. He
knew two things that would definitely help make his
friend happy again: football and fun.

After training one day, Antoine and Paul put on a
skills show for the crowd. They passed the ball back
and forth, using all their best flicks and tricks.

'That's more like it, Grizi!'

By the time the tournament started, Antoine's
champion spirit had returned and he was back to
his usual smiling self. He couldn't wait to represent
his country and make the people proud. In front of
75,000 fans, and against Romania, Olivier rolled the

ball to Antoine, who passed it back to N'Golo Kanté. Euro 2016 was officially underway!

With Romania sitting deep in defence, France created lots of chances. Olivier headed wide from Dimitri's cross, and then Antoine somehow headed the ball against the post from close range.

'How did I miss that?' he cried up at the sky.

It was another glorious chance missed, and another disappointing day for Antoine. As soon as France were winning, Deschamps decided to take him off.

'Don't worry, we've got plenty more matches ahead of us,' his manager told him.

For the second match against Albania, however, Deschamps dropped Antoine to the subs bench. He had to sit there impatiently as France failed to score again and again.

'Get me out there!' he wanted to scream, but instead, he waited his turn.

When Antoine finally raced onto the pitch, time was running out. A 0–0 draw would be a disastrous result. They simply had to score!

In the penalty area, Antoine never stopped moving. One second he was at the front post, and the next he was at the back post. The Albania defenders tried their best to mark him, but it was impossible! As Adil Rami crossed the ball into the box with seconds to go, Antoine was in the perfect position – in between the two centre-backs. He steered his header down into the bottom corner. *1–0!*

Goooooooooooooooooooooaaaaaaaaaaaaaaaaallllllllllllll llllllllllllll!!!!!!!!!!!!!!!!!!!!!

Antoine had never experienced so many different emotions at once: passion, pride, frustration, relief and joy all mixed together.

'Come on!' he roared as his teammates surrounded him.

It felt so great to finally be France's hero, saving the day from the subs bench. Antoine had his confidence back! From that massive moment on, he became the star of Euro 2016.

In the Round of 16, Antoine powered a brilliant header past the Republic of Ireland goalkeeper, and then added a second with his lethal left foot.

MATT AND TOM OLDFIELD

Gooooooooooooooooooooaaaaaaaaaaaaaaaaaaallllllllllll llllllllllllllll!!!!!!!!!!!!!!!!!!!!

'You're on fire, Grizi!' Dimitri shouted after kissing his magic boot.

In the quarter-final against Iceland, Antoine made two assists for Paul and Dimitri, and then scored a goal of his own with a cheeky chip.

Gooooooooooooooooooooaaaaaaaaaaaaaaaaaaallllllllllll llllllllllllllll!!!!!!!!!!!!!!!!!!!!

With a wide grin across his face, he did his 'Hotline Bling' dance for the cheering fans. Antoine was really enjoying himself now.

Next up, however, was a big semi-final against Germany – not only the tournament favourites, but also the team that had knocked France out of the 2014 World Cup. *Les Bleus* were going to need Antoine more than ever...

In the last minute of the first half, the referee awarded France a penalty. What a chance to take the lead! But would Antoine be brave enough to take it after his miss in the Champions League final? Of course he would! There were no doubts

in his mind. His team needed him, and he wasn't
going to let them down. As he calmly put the
ball down on the spot, the people of France held
their breaths.

Pressure, what pressure? Manuel Neuer dived
to his left, and Antoine placed the penalty kick to
his right.

*Goooooooooooooooooooaaaaaaaaaaaaaaaalllllllllllll
lllllllllllll!!!!!!!!!!!!!!!!!!!*

Antoine couldn't stop scoring. In the second half,
he reacted quickly to poke the ball past Neuer again.
2–0 – game over!

After the full-time whistle, the France players
celebrated together in front of their supporters. They
had beaten the World Champions, Germany, and
they were through to the final of Euro 2016!

Allez Les Bleus! Allez Les Bleus! Allez Les Bleus!

Although it had been a real team effort, Antoine
was now France's main man. With six goals, he was
the top scorer in the whole tournament. He was also
a national hero with a cool new nickname.

'Zizou' had won the World Cup for France in

1998 and eighteen years later, 'Grizou' was about to win Euro 2016 for France.

'No pressure then, Grizou!' Paul joked.

In the Euro 2016 Final, it was France vs Portugal, the country where Antoine's grandparents had grown up. It was also a battle of the superstars – Antoine vs Cristiano Ronaldo. Both players were only one match away from making their international dream come true.

Ronaldo's big day only lasted twenty-five minutes. He hobbled off the pitch in tears with a bad knee injury. Portugal had lost their leader. Surely, the stage was now set for Antoine to win the Euros for France? In the first half, however, he hardly had a chance.

'Come on, Grizou!' Patrice Evra yelled at half-time. 'We need you!'

Antoine was determined to do better in the second half. He dribbled through and shot from the left side of the box, but Rui Patrício made an easy save.

'Unlucky, keep going!' Paul encouraged him.

With thirty minutes to go, Antoine made a clever run between the Portugal defenders to meet Kingsley

Coman's cross. Surely, this was it – the moment that the whole French nation was waiting for.

Antoine jumped up and won the header, but the ball whizzed just over the crossbar. What? How? The fans couldn't believe it, and neither could he.

'Noooooooooooo!' he groaned with his hands on his head. 'How did I miss *that?*'

Antoine had wasted a golden chance to win the final for France. He just had to hope that he would get another opportunity before it was too late...

Unfortunately, it was Portugal's sub striker Eder who scored the winning goal in extra-time. As he watched the ball hit the back of the net, Antoine's shoulders slumped. Was he about to lose another important final? Yes, the final whistle blew, and Portugal were the winners!

Antoine had come so close to achieving his Euro 2016 dream. So close and yet so far. This time, he didn't cry, like he had done when they lost to Germany at the 2014 World Cup. He was older now and more experienced. If he wanted to be France's superstar, he needed to show his teammates that he could be a strong leader.

'This time, we tried and failed,' he comforted them. 'But next time, we're going to succeed!'

Soon, it would be trophy time again. The disappointments only made Antoine more determined than ever.

CHAPTER 21

TROPHY TIME
AT LAST!

Despite France losing in the final, Euro 2016 was
still a massive moment in Antoine's career. 'Grizi'
had become 'Grizou', a national hero and an
international superstar. He won the tournament's
Best Player and Top Goalscorer awards and he even
came in third place for the Ballon d'Or. There were
now only two better footballers in the whole wide
world: Ronaldo and Messi.

'And you're way younger than both of them!' his
proud brother, Theo, reminded him.

After a relaxing holiday back home in Mâcon,
Antoine returned to Madrid, ready to shine again.
Unfortunately, however, the 2016–17 season was

the same old story. Atlético were knocked out in the semi-finals of the Spanish Cup by Messi's Barcelona and then in the semi-finals of the Champions League by Ronaldo's Real Madrid, before finishing third behind both clubs in La Liga.

'I'm fed up with losing to those guys,' Antoine moaned. 'We need to find a way to win something. Anything!'

Antoine had been Atleti's top scorer for three years in a row, but it was clear that he needed more support in attack. Even superstars couldn't get all the goals on their own!

Did the club have enough money to sign a second superstar? If not, Antoine would have to consider his other options. He wouldn't go to Atleti's rivals Barcelona or Real Madrid, but Manchester United were offering him the chance to play in the Premier League with Paul.

'Grizi, you'd love it here!' his friend promised him.

It was tempting, but Antoine wasn't ready to abandon Atlético just yet. He loved the club and he couldn't leave without winning something first. He decided to stay for one more season and if they still hadn't won a trophy, then he would think about moving on.

His Atleti teammates were delighted. 'Great, this is going to be our year,' Saúl announced confidently. 'I can feel it!'

But by December 2017, their season was turning into a disaster. Atlético were already a long way behind Barcelona in the Spanish League and they were out of the Champions League too.

So, Simeone and his players had to switch to Trophy Plan B: the Europa League. Atleti had won it twice before, in 2010 and 2012. It was time for them to complete the hat-trick.

'It won't be easy,' their captain Gabi warned, 'but it's our best shot at winning a trophy!'

Antoine was ready to light up the Europa League, and finally, he had a new star strike partner. Diego Costa was back at Atlético after a successful spell at Chelsea.

'Did you miss me?' he joked on his first day at training.

'Not really,' Koke said with a smile, 'but you and Grizi are a match made in heaven!'

Diego's nickname was 'The Beast' because he was big and strong, and because it was a very bad idea to make him angry. His power, combined with Antoine's pace and skill, would make Atlético better than ever.

Once their Europa League campaign started, Antoine couldn't stop scoring.

He chased after Yannick's through-ball and coolly nutmegged the keeper.

Goooooooooooooooooooaaaaaaaaaaaaaaaaallllllllllllll llllllllllllllll!!!!!!!!!!!!!!!!!!!

Atlético Madrid 5 Copenhagen 1

He got the ball on the edge of the box and chipped a curling shot into the top corner.

Goooooooooooooooooooaaaaaaaaaaaaaaaaallllllllllllll llllllllllllllll!!!!!!!!!!!!!!!!!!!

Atlético Madrid 8 Lokomotiv Moscow 1

He pounced on a defender's mistake and dribbled into the penalty area.

Goooooooooooooooooooaaaaaaaaaaaaaaaaallllllllllllll llllllllllllllll!!!!!!!!!!!!!!!!!!!

Atlético Madrid 2 Sporting Lisbon 1

'Griezmann is far too good for that competition!'
some people argued but Antoine wasn't listening.
He was fully focused on getting to the Europa
League Final, and then winning it. That's all he
cared about.

The games were getting tougher and tougher,
however. In the semi-finals, Atlético faced Arsenal.
In the first leg in London, Antoine's France teammate
Alexandre Lacazette opened the scoring for The
Gunners but Atlético never gave up. They were
the masters of knock-out cup football, and they
knew the importance of scoring an away goal...

Antoine chased after a long ball over the top
and used his strength to shrug off another France
teammate, Laurent Koscielny. He was into the
penalty area with just the Arsenal goalkeeper to
beat. His first shot was blocked but he scored the
rebound.

*Goooooooooooooooooooooaaaaaaaaaaaaaaaaalllllllllllll
lllllllllllllll!!!!!!!!!!!!!!!!!!!!!*

What an important strike that would turn out

to be! Antoine ran over to the Atlético fans and did his Fortnite dance for them. Making the letter 'L' on his forehead, he swung his legs from side to side joyfully. Then he turned to celebrate with his teammates.

'Come on!' he roared.

The second leg was played at Atlético's brand-new Wanda Metropolitano Stadium. The atmosphere was electric from start to finish. The club was one win away from another big European final, and the fans cheered them on to victory.

Atleti! Atleti! Atleti!

Just before half-time, Atlético's superstar strike partners scored a great goal together. Antoine got the ball on the right and played a perfect pass into Diego's path. His powerful shot flicked up off the goalkeeper and into the roof of the net.

Atlético Madrid 2 Arsenal 1!

'Yes, Grizi, we did it!' Diego cheered.

That turned out to be the winning goal – Atlético were through to the Europa League Final!

For Antoine, it would be a journey back home.

The match would be against Marseille at the Parc Olympique Lyonnais. That was the new home of Lyon – the club that he had supported as a kid, and the club that had rejected him.

'We've got to win now!' he told his teammates.

It was time for Antoine to shine brightly like a true superstar. So far, he had failed to do so in his two big finals: the 2016 Champions League final with Atlético, and then the Euro 2016 final with France. But now, Antoine was ready to show what a big game player he had become.

As soon as the match kicked off, he was alert and on the move. If there was even half a chance to score, Antoine was going to find it! After twenty minutes, the Marseille goalkeeper played a risky pass to Zambo Anguissa, who let the ball bobble over his foot. In a flash, Gabi gave it to Antoine and this time, he wasn't going to miss.

Gooooooooooooooooooooaaaaaaaaaaaaaaaaallllllllllll llllllllllllll!!!!!!!!!!!!!!!!!!!!

Atlético, and Antoine, were off to the perfect start. After a quick Fortnite dance, it was hugs all round.

'Grizi, can you please get a new goal celebration?'
Gabi joked. 'That one's rubbish!'

'No way, it's my thing!'

Just after half-time, Antoine was 'Taking the L'
again. He passed to Koke and then raced forward for
the one-two. Antoine dribbled the ball into the box
and at the last second, he lifted it delicately over the
diving keeper.

*Goooooooooooooooooooaaaaaaaaaaaaaaaalllllllllllll
lllllllllllll!!!!!!!!!!!!!!!!!!!*

'Yes, Grizi!' Koke cried out as they bumped fists.

Two strikes in the final – what a superstar
performance!

It was soon game over, and Atlético were the 2018
Europa League winners! At the final whistle, the
players laughed and danced and sang.

Campeones, Campeones, Olé! Olé! Olé!

For Antoine, it was triple trophy time. He had
also won the Man of the Match award *and* the
Best Player of the Tournament prize. The one that
mattered most, however, was the team trophy.
Having collected his winners' medal, Antoine

couldn't wait any longer. He lent forward and gave the cup a quick kiss.

'Hey, I haven't even lifted it yet!' Gabi teased him.

'Sorry, captain!'

Antoine stood with his strike partner Diego as Gabi got ready to raise the trophy high into the Lyon sky. Three, two, one…

Hurraaaaaaaaay!!!!

Atleti! Atleti! Atleti!

CHAPTER 22

WORLD CUP WINNER!

As the Atlético players paraded the Europa League trophy around the pitch in Lyon, there was only one month to go until the 2018 World Cup in Russia.

Antoine counted down the days. He had never been so excited about a tournament in his life. France had come so close to winning Euro 2016 and now, two years later, their team was even better. They had so many talented young players, and especially in attack. Thomas Lemar was twenty-two years old, Ousmane Dembélé was twenty-one, and Kylian Mbappé was only nineteen.

'Man, you guys make me feel so old!' Antoine moaned as the players arrived for the training camp at Clairefontaine.

'What are you talking about, Grizi?' Paul joked.
'You might be twenty-seven, but you behave like a
seven-year-old!'

'Whatever, Piochi. You're just jealous because
my goal celebration is better than your silly 'Dab'
dance!'

Antoine and Paul were senior players now and
two of France's leaders, both on and off the pitch.
With their pranks and selfies, they made sure that
everyone was smiling and laughing ahead of the
main event.

'A happy team is a successful team!' their manager,
Deschamps, liked to say.

The fans were just as excited about the World Cup
as the players. They couldn't wait to watch Kylian
racing down the wing, but they knew that the team's
main trophy hopes rested with 'Grizou'. Thanks to
his many hairstyles, his cool celebrations and his
match-winning goals, Antoine was the most popular
man in France.

'Good luck, Grizou!' the supporters shouted as

the squad set off for Russia. 'Bring that World Cup trophy home!'

That was Antoine's aim. He was going to lead France all the way to another final and this time, they wouldn't lose.

'Let's do this!' he told Paul.

With a massive month of football ahead of them, France started slowly. In their first match against Australia, they only really got going in the second half. Paul slid a great pass through to Antoine and as he dribbled into the box, a defender tripped him up.

'Penalty!' Antoine cried out.

At first, the referee shook his head but after checking with VAR, he eventually pointed to the spot. Antoine stepped up and...

Goooooooooooooooooooooaaaaaaaaaaaaaaaaalllllllllllll lllllllllllllll!!!!!!!!!!!!!!!!!!!!

He was off the mark already!

'Yes, Grizi!' Ousmane cheered, giving Antoine a big hug.

Australia equalised but with ten minutes to go, Paul's shot bounced down off the crossbar and over the goal line. *2–1!*

'Yes, Piochi!' Antoine screamed, jumping to his feet on the subs bench. What a relief!

France never gave up; that's what made them such a terrific team. Against Peru, Antoine, Paul and Raphaël Varane all missed good chances to score. They didn't panic, though. Paul won the ball in midfield and played it to Olivier. His shot was going in but Kylian made sure. *1–0!*

Kylian ran over to the France fans to do his trademark celebration. Who else loved a goal celebration? Antoine! He stood next to Kylian and copied his moves:

1. Jump to a stop,

2. Fold your arms across your chest,

3. Look as cool as possible.

'I still prefer my Fortnite dance!' Antoine said with a smile.

Kylian's tap-in was enough to send France through to the World Cup Round of 16. So far, so good. Antoine felt like he was still just getting started.

'I'm saving myself for the big games!' he told Paul.

The first of those came against Argentina. The South Americans weren't playing well but, in Messi, they had the best player in the world, plus deadly forwards Ángel Di María and Sergio Agüero.

'Don't you dare underestimate them!' Deschamps told the French players in the dressing room. 'I need you all to stay fully focused until the final whistle.'

Antoine was determined to win the battle of the superstars. When Kylian won a free kick, Antoine grabbed the ball straight away.

'This one's mine,' he told Paul confidently.

'Go for it, Grizi!'

Antoine struck his shot sweetly and it curled up over the Argentina wall and towards the top corner. The keeper hadn't even moved but sadly, the ball bounced back off the crossbar. *So close!*

Five minutes later, Antoine got a second chance to score. Kylian used his electric pace to dribble past three defenders, before being fouled in the box. *Penalty!* Antoine stepped up and…

Goooooooooooooooooooaaaaaaaaaaaaaaaaallllllllllll

IIIIIIIIIIIIIIII!!!!!!!!!!!!!!!!!!!!!!

As Antoine ran towards the corner flag, he was already making the 'L' sign up above his head. The fans in the stadium copied his Fortnite dance, but Kylian refused.

'No way, I'm not making a fool of myself, mate!'

Antoine carried on working hard for his team, at both ends of the pitch. He chased all the way back to tackle Messi in his own penalty area. The France supporters chanted their hero's nickname:

'Grizou! Grizou! Grizou!'

It was Kylian who stole the show, however. In the second half, he scored two great goals to win the game for France.

'Kyky, what a finish!' Antoine cried out.

He wasn't jealous at all. Winning was a team effort, and France were lucky enough to have a squad full of superstars.

So, who would their hero be, in the World Cup quarter-final against Uruguay? France's attack was taking on the deadliest defence in the tournament: Diego Godín and José Giménez. Antoine knew them very well because they both played with him at Atlético Madrid.

'Trust me, we'll need to be at our absolute best to beat them,' Antoine told Kylian and Olivier before kick-off.

With time running out in the first half, it was still 0–0. France won a free kick wide on the right and Antoine stood ready to take it. He faked to strike it once, and then *BANG!* The nation held their breath as the ball curled beautifully into the box. Raphaël ran towards it and headed it down into the bottom corner. *1–0!*

'*Allez Les Bleus!*'

Antoine punched the air passionately. He had set up the opening goal and soon he would be scoring one of his own.

When he got the ball on the left wing, Antoine looked up to see who was waiting for one of his dangerous deliveries. But he could only see Kylian, a long way away near the back post…

Suddenly, Antoine had an idea: if everyone was expecting a cross, why not surprise them with a shot?

BANG! He blasted the ball with plenty of power and it slipped straight through the Uruguay keeper's gloves.

Goooooooooooooooooooaaaaaaaaaaaaaaaaaallllllllllll llllllllllllll!!!!!!!!!!!!!!!!!!!!

Another big game goal for 'Grizou'! This time, Antoine didn't celebrate with his trademark dance. He decided that it wouldn't be fair to his Uruguayan friends, Diego and José. But inside, the adrenaline was buzzing because France were into the semi-finals!

As the team prepared for their next match, Antoine practised lots and lots of free kicks and corner-kicks. Set-pieces had become a really important weapon at the World Cup. England, for example, were scoring loads of headers, thanks to Kieran Trippier's excellent crosses.

People were calling Trippier 'The New Beckham', but surely that was Antoine? His cross had already created one goal for Raphaël against Uruguay. Could he set up another to help France beat Belgium in the semi-final?

It was a tight game between two brilliant teams.
Belgium had the skill of Eden Hazard, the strength of
Romelu Lukaku, and the vision of Kevin De Bruyne.
France, meanwhile, had the pace of Kylian, the
power of Paul and Antoine's ace left foot.

Early in the second half, Antoine curled in a
teasing corner and Samuel Umtiti flicked it on. *1–0
to France!*

The centre-back did his own celebration dance and
this time, everyone joined in: Antoine, Paul, Raphaël,
even Kylian.

'We're nearly there now, lads,' their captain, Hugo,
shouted out from goal. 'No silly mistakes, okay? Stay
focused!'

France defended magnificently. Antoine ran and
ran, making tackles in midfield and then leading his
team forward on the counter-attack. Although they
didn't quite score a second, they didn't let any goals
in either.

At the final whistle, Antoine fell to the floor and
raised his fists to the sky. 'Yessssss!' he cried out

joyfully. 'We did it – we're in the World Cup final!'

The big day soon arrived – France vs Luka Modrić's Croatia. There were 78,000 fans watching in the stadium, and millions more back home. Antoine thought about his family, his friends, and his second father, the Real Sociedad scout, Éric Olhats. He wanted to win the World Cup for all of them and he would never get a better chance.

In the seventeenth minute, Antoine won a free kick in a good position for France. What a chance! He curled another incredible cross into the six-yard box and Raphaël made a late run and leap to reach it. He couldn't, but the ball bounced off the head of Antoine's old Atlético teammate, Mario Mandžukić, instead. *Own goal – 1–0 to France!*

'Yes, yes, YES!' Antoine roared as he skidded across the grass on his knees. It was another key assist to add to his collection. They were on their way to World Cup glory…

Twenty minutes later, he got a goal to go with that assist. When France won a penalty, Antoine stepped up and...

*Goooooooooooooooooooaaaaaaaaaaaaaaaaalllllllllllll
llllllllllllllll!!!!!!!!!!!!!!!!!!!!!*

He had learnt his lesson from that Champions
League final; he never lost his cool anymore. Antoine
was Mr Calm and Mr Confident. Midway through
the second half, he did a couple of keep-uppies in the
box and then laid the ball back to Paul. His right-
foot shot was blocked, so he tried again with his left.
GOAL – 3–1!

'Yes, Piochi!' Antoine cheered.

Surely, that was game over? Just in case Croatia
were planning an incredible comeback, Kylian made
sure with a stunning long-range strike. *4–1!*

'Yes, Kyky!' Antoine screamed.

At last, the full-time whistle blew, and France were
the 2018 World Cup winners!

'We did it!' Antoine shouted, hugging his best
friend, Paul. 'We're national heroes now!'

It was a night of jubilant celebrations, both there
in Russia and back home in France.

Antoine wasn't sure that the smile would ever

leave his face. The little football-mad boy from Mâcon had worked so hard for this moment. He had never given up – not even when everyone said he was too small to be a star, and not even when it looked like he would never lift a top trophy.

And now, his ultimate dream had come true. Not only was he a World Cup winner, but he was also the Man of the Match in the World Cup Final, with a goal and two assists. Move over Messi and Ronaldo: Antoine was now the best big game player in the world!

ANTOINE GRIEZMANN HONOURS

Real Sociedad
🏆 Segunda División: 2009–10

Atlético Madrid
🏆 Spanish Super Cup: 2014
🏆 UEFA Europa League: 2017–18
🏆 UEFA Super Cup: 2018

France
🏆 UEFA European Under-19 Championship: 2010
🏆 FIFA World Cup: 2018

Individual

🏆 UEFA European Under-19 Championship Team of the Tournament: 2010

🏆 Onze d'Or French Player of the Year: 2014–15

🏆 UEFA La Liga Team of the Season: 2015–16

🏆 La Liga Best Player: 2016

🏆 French Player of the Year: 2016

🏆 UEFA European Championship Player of the Tournament: 2016

🏆 UEFA European Championship Golden Boot: 2016

🏆 UEFA Team of the Year: 2016

🏆 UEFA Europa League Player of the Season: 2017–18

🏆 FIFA World Cup top assist provider: 2018

🏆 FIFA World Cup Silver Boot: 2018

GRIEZMANN

17 **THE FACTS**

NAME: ANTOINE GRIEZMANN

DATE OF BIRTH: 21 March 1991

AGE: 29

PLACE OF BIRTH: Mâcon

NATIONALITY: French

BEST FRIEND: Paul Pogba

CURRENT CLUB: FC Barcelona

POSITION: Centre-Forward (CF)

THE STATS

Height (cm):	174
Club appearances:	496
Club goals:	199
Club trophies:	4
International appearances:	78
International goals:	30
International trophies:	2
Ballon d'Ors:	0

★ ★ ★ **HERO RATING: 89** ★ ★ ★

GREATEST MOMENTS

20 AUGUST 2013,
LYON 0–2 REAL SOCIEDAD

This was the night when Antoine first went from star to superstar. Having helped Sociedad to finish fourth in La Liga, he then got them into the Champions League Group Stage with a win over Lyon. Back in France at the club who had rejected him as a boy, Antoine leapt into the air to score a spectacular scissor-kick.

13 APRIL 2016,
ATLÉTICO MADRID 2–0 BARCELONA

Three years on from that scissor-kick, Antoine helped lead Atlético all the way to the Champions League final. Eventually, they lost to Ronaldo's Real Madrid – but before that, they beat Messi's Barcelona. That night, Antoine was the hero, scoring both goals – a header and then a penalty.

7 JULY 2016,
FRANCE 2–0 GERMANY

After a slow start, Antoine became the star of Euro 2016. He scored France's winner against Albania, then two against Republic of Ireland, one against Iceland and then two in this semi-final against the World Champions, Germany. They weren't Antoine's best goals, but he had proved himself at the highest level.

16 MAY 2018,
MARSEILLE 0–3 ATLÉTICO MADRID

Antoine's successful summer of 2018 began with the
Europa League Final. He had scored four times in the
tournament already, and he added two more that night
in Lyon. After losing in the Champions League and Euro
finals in 2016, at last Antoine showed the world that
he was a big game player after all. And there were even
greater achievements ahead…

15 JULY 2018,
FRANCE 4–2 CROATIA

Antoine had a wonderful 2018 World Cup, saving his
best performance for the final. He set up France's first
goal with a fantastic free kick, scored the second from
the penalty spot, and then assisted Paul Pogba for the
third. Antoine was Man of the Match and made sure
that he would stay a national hero forever.

PLAY LIKE YOUR HEROES

ANTOINE GRIEZMANN'S DANGEROUS DELIVERIES

STEP 1: Practise, practise, practise!

STEP 2: When your team wins a free kick, grab the ball. This is yours; everyone else can back off!

STEP 3: Make sure you send all your biggest players into the box. The more the merrier.

STEP 4: Pick your target – are you aiming for Pete near the penalty spot, or Simon in the six-yard box? Either way, you need to be accurate.

STEP 5: Wait with your hands on your hips. Once the referee blows the whistle, take a couple of short steps towards the ball and then *BANG!*

STEP 6: Put plenty of power and curl on your cross. That way, even the slightest flick might lead to a...

STEP 7: *GOAL!* For you, an assist feels as good as scoring a goal, if not better. I hope you've got a good celebration dance!

TEST YOUR KNOWLEDGE

1. Name at least two of Antoine's childhood football heroes.

2. Which country did Antoine's grandad want him to play for?

3. Which team was Antoine on trial at when he was scouted by Éric Olhats?

4. How old was Antoine when he moved from France to Spain?

5. What was Antoine's first senior trophy?

6. How much did Atlético Madrid pay to sign Antoine in 2014?

7. Which team did Antoine score his first Champions League goal against?

8. What nickname did the French fans give Antoine during Euro 2016?

9. What trophy did Antoine win in May 2018 with Atlético Madrid?

10. What's the name of Antoine's Fortnite dance goal celebration?

11. How many goals has Antoine scored in his last two major international tournaments, Euro 2016 and World Cup 2018?

Answers below. . . No cheating!

MBAPPE

TABLE OF CONTENTS

CHAPTER 1

FROM RUSSIA
WITH LOVE

On 14 July 2018, Kylian sent a message to his millions of social media followers, from Russia with love: 'Happy French national day everyone. Let's hope the party continues until tomorrow night!'

'Tomorrow night' – 15 July – the French national team would be playing in the World Cup final at the Luzhniki Stadium in Moscow. It was the most important football match on the planet and Kylian's country was counting on him.

So far, he hadn't let them down at all. In fact, Kylian had been France's speedy superstar, scoring the winning goal against Denmark, and then two more in an amazing man-of-the-match performance against Argentina. That all made him the nation's best 'Number 10' since Zinedine Zidane back in 1998.

That was the year that France last won the World Cup.

That was also the year that Kylian was born.

Thanks to their new young superstar, '*Les Bleus*' were now the favourites to lift the famous golden trophy again. They had already beaten Lionel Messi's Argentina, Luis Suárez's Uruguay in the quarter-finals, and Eden Hazard's Belgium in the semi-finals. Now, the only nation standing in their way was Luka Modrić's Croatia.

'You've done so well to get this far,' the France manager, Didier Deschamps, told them as kick-off approached and the nerves began to jangle. 'Now, you just need to go out there and finish off the job!'

A massive 'Yeah!' echoed around the room. It was one big team effort, from captain Hugo Lloris in goal through to Kylian, Antoine Griezmann and Olivier Giroud in attack. Everyone worked hard and everyone worked together.

By the way, those jangling nerves didn't

belong to Kylian. No way, he was the coolest character around! He never let anything faze him. When he was younger, he hadn't just hoped to play in a World Cup final; he had expected it. It was all part of his killer plan to conquer the football world.

Out on the pitch for the final in Moscow, Kylian sang the words of the French national anthem with a big smile on his face. As a four-year-old, some people had laughed at his ambitious dreams. Well, they definitely weren't laughing now.

'Right, let's do this!' Paul Pogba clapped and cheered as they took up their positions. His partnership with Kylian would be key for France. Whenever Paul got the ball in midfield, he would look to find his pacy teammate with a perfect pass.

Kylian's first action of the final, however, was in defence. He rushed back quickly to block a Croatia cross.

'Well done!' France's centre-back Samuel Umtiti shouted.

Once that was done, it was all about attacking.

Even in a World Cup final, Kylian wasn't afraid to try his tricks and flicks. They didn't always work but it was worth the risk.

It was an end-to-end first half, full of exciting action. First, Antoine curled in a dangerous free kick and Mario Mandžukić headed the ball into his own net. 1–0 to France! Kylian punched the air – what a start!

Ivan Perišić equalised for Croatia but then he handballed it in his own box. Penalty! Antoine stepped up... and scored – 2–1 to France!

The players were happy to hear the half-time whistle blow. They needed a break to breathe and regroup. Although France were winning, they still had work to do if they wanted to become World Champions again.

'We need to calm things down and take control of the game,' Deschamps told his players. 'Stay smart out there!'

Kylian listened carefully to his manager's message. He needed to relax and play to his strengths – his skill but also his speed. This was his chance to go down in World Cup history:

Pelé in 1958,

Diego Maradona in 1986,

Zidane in 1998,

Ronaldo in 2002,

Kylian in 2018?

In the second half, France's superstars shone much more brightly. Kylian collected Paul's long pass and sprinted straight past the Croatia centre-back. Was he about to score in his first World Cup final? No, the keeper came out to make a good save.

'Ohhhh!' the supporters groaned in disappointment.

But a few minutes later, Paul and Kylian linked up again. From wide on the right wing, Kylian dribbled towards goal. Uh oh, the Croatia left-back was in big trouble.

With a stepover and a little hop, Kylian cut inside towards goal but in a flash, he fooled the defender with another quick change of direction.

'Go on!' the France fans urged their exciting young hero.

What next? Kylian still had two defenders in front

of him, so he pulled it back to Antoine instead. He couldn't find a way through either so he passed it on to Paul. Paul's first shot was blocked but his second flew into the bottom corner. 3–1!

Kylian threw his arms up in the air and then ran over to congratulate his friend. Surely, France had one hand on the World Cup trophy now.

Antoine had scored, and so had Paul. That meant it must be Kylian's turn next! He would have to score soon, however, in case Deschamps decided to take him off early...

When he received the pass from Lucas Hernández, Kylian was in the middle of the pitch, at least ten yards outside the penalty area. Was he too far out to shoot? No, there was no such thing as 'too far' for Kylian! He shifted the ball to the right and then BANG! He tucked the ball into the bottom corner before the keeper could even dive. 4–1!

Goooooooooooooooooooooaaaaaaaaaaaaaaaallllllllllll lllllllllllllll!!!!!!!!!!!!!!!!!!!

As his teammates rushed over to him, Kylian had just enough time for his trademark celebration. With a little jump, he planted his feet, folded his arms across his chest, and tried to look as cool as he could. That last part was really hard because he had just scored in a World Cup final!

The next thirty minutes ticked by very slowly but eventually, the game was over. France 4 Croatia 2 – they were the 2018 World Champions!

Allez Les Bleus! Allez Les Bleus! Allez Les Bleus!

Kylian used the last of his energy to race around the pitch, handing out hugs to everyone he saw: his sad opponents, his happy teammates, his manager, EVERYONE! In that amazing moment, he would have hugged every single French person in the world if he could. Instead, he blew kisses at the cameras. From Russia with love!

And Kylian's incredible night wasn't over yet. Wearing his country's flag around his waist, he walked up on stage to collect the tournament's Best Young Player award from Emmanuel Macron.

'Thank you, you're a national hero now!' the French President told him proudly.

'My pleasure, Sir!' Kylian replied.

Would his smile ever fade? Certainly not while he had a World Cup winners' medal around his neck and the beautiful World Cup trophy in his hands. He didn't ever want to let go. Kylian kissed it and raised it high into the Moscow night sky.

'Hurray!' the fans cheered for him.

At the age of nineteen, Kylian was already living out his wildest dreams. The boy from Bondy had become a World Cup winner and football's next great superstar.

CHAPTER 2

A SPORTY FAMILY IN A SPORTY SUBURB

'What if he doesn't like sports?' Wilfried Mbappé whispered to his wife, Fayza Lamari, as they watched their new-born son, Kylian, sleeping peacefully in his cot. He was a man who loved to laugh but at that moment, he had a worried look on his face.

Fayza smiled and spoke softly so as not to wake the baby. 'Does it really matter? Kylian can do whatever he wants to do, and we're going to love him no matter what!'

Her husband nodded but she could still see the frown lines on his forehead.

'Relax, Wilfried, he's our son, so of course he's going to LOVE sports!'

With parents like his, Kylian was always destined
to be a sporting superstar.

Wilfried's favourite sport was football. When
he was younger, he had moved to France from
Cameroon in order to find a good job. As well as
that, Wilfried had also been lucky enough to find
the two loves of his life – his wife, Fayza, and his
local football club, AS Bondy. His playing days
were now over, but he had become a youth team
coach instead.

Fayza's favourite sport was handball. She was a
star player for AS Bondy in France's top division. Ever
since she was a kid, Fayza had been racing up and
down the right wing, competing fiercely with her
rivals. She couldn't wait to get back out on the court,
now that Kylian was born.

'No-one messes with your mum!' Wilfried always
told his sons proudly.

Not only were the Mbappés a very sporty
family, but they also lived in a very sporty suburb of
Paris. Over the years, so many successful athletes,
basketball players and footballers had grown up in

Bondy. There was top talent on display wherever you turned!

The sports club, AS Bondy, was at the heart of the local community, right in the middle of all the shops and tower blocks. Growing up, Kylian could see the local stadium from the windows of their apartment. It was an inspiring sight.

AS Bondy was a place where people from lots of different French-speaking backgrounds – Algeria, Morocco, Tunisia, Haiti, Togo, Mali, Senegal, Ivory Coast – could come together and enjoy themselves. That was really important because life wasn't easy for the local people. They had to work long hours in order to feed their families and strive towards a brighter future.

For the young people of Bondy, the sports club was particularly special. It was their home away from home, where they could develop their skills, while at the same time staying out of trouble. Coaches like Wilfried taught them three simple rules to live by:

1) Respect each other.

2) Stay humble.

3) Love sport.

At AS Bondy, youngsters could forget about their problems and just focus on their sporting dreams.

In years to come, the local kids would look up at a big mural showing Kylian's face under the words, 'Bondy: Ville Des Possibles'. No, it wasn't the wealthiest part of Paris, but it was a 'City of Possibilities' where, with hard work and dedication, you could achieve your dreams.

So, what was Kylian's sporting dream? To play handball like his mother, or football like his father? His adopted older brother, Jirés Kembo Ekoko, was already the star of Wilfried's Under-10s football team. Would Kylian follow in his footsteps?

Or perhaps Kylian would choose to play a different sport...

'He can do whatever he wants to do,' Fayza reminded Wilfried, 'and we're going to love him no matter what!'

Growing up, Kylian enjoyed playing tennis and basketball with his friends, but there was really only one sport for him. To his dad's delight, that sport turned out to be football!

CHAPTER 3

THE LITTLE PRINCE OF BONDY

Little Kylian didn't know the meaning of the word 'slow'. He was a football hero in a hurry.

By the age of two, he was already a familiar face in the AS Bondy dressing room. Just as the players were preparing for the match ahead, a little boy would race in with a football tucked under his arm.

'Look who it is – our mascot, the Little Prince of Bondy!' the club president, Atmane Airouche greeted him. 'You're just in time for the team-talk!'

Even if Wilfried wasn't there with him, Kylian was never any trouble. When the manager was talking, he just sat there quietly next to the Bondy players and listened. Before they went out onto the pitch, they all high-fived him. He was their good luck charm.

'Are we going to win today?' the captain asked Kylian.

He nodded eagerly. 'Yeah!'

Kylian would then go out and watch the games with a football at his feet.

By the age of six, Kylian already had his own future all planned out.

'What do you want to be when you're older?' Wilfried asked, recording his son's reply.

'I want to be a footballer,' Kylian said, looking confidently at the video camera. 'I'm going to play for France and I'm going to play in the World Cup too.'

Fayza tried very hard not to laugh at the serious expression on her son's young face. He had such amazing ambition! As the French national anthem played, Kylian sang along with his hand on his heart, just like the players he saw on TV.

'Great, and what club would you like to play for?'

'Bondy!'

Kylian was already training with the juniors. His

coach, Antonio Riccardi, was one of Wilfried and Fayza's closest friends, and so he had been kicking balls around with their sons for years. However, this was the first time that he would see Kylian playing a proper match against kids his own age.

'Wow!' was Antonio's response.

He looked so tiny in his baggy green shirt and shorts, but boy, could Kylian play football!

Even during the warm-up, Antonio could see the difference. He was so much better than everyone else. For a young kid, he really seemed to understand the game. Kylian didn't just kick and chase, like the others; he thought about what he wanted to do with the ball, and then did it. All those weekends at Bondy, spent watching and listening to the adults around him... Kylian had been taking everything in.

'Right, let's practise our dribbling!' Antonio called out.

The coach had set up a line of cones for them to weave through before taking a shot at goal. It looked easy but it wasn't. The first four kids either took it too fast or too slow. They either bumped the ball off cone after cone, or crawled their way down the line like a sleepy tortoise.

'At that speed, you're going to get tackled every time!' Antonio told them as kindly as he could.

At last, it was Kylian's turn and he couldn't wait to show off his skills. He had been working hard on his dribbling at home with his dad and Jirés. It was now time to test himself in front of a bigger audience.

One, two, three, four – as Kylian raced through the cones, the ball stayed stuck to his right foot. His control was so good that he didn't knock a single one of them.

'Excellent!' Antonio called out. 'Now shoot!'

But by then, Kylian was already rushing over to collect his ball from the back of the net. His shot hit the top-left corner of the net before the goalkeeper had even moved.

Kylian was the standout player in the passing practice too. The touch, the movement, the accuracy – it was like he was a professional already! Antonio was blown away by the Little Prince of Bondy. He had coached a lot of impressive kids in Paris, but he had never seen a six-year-old with that much footballing talent. Never!

'Surely he's too good to play with kids his own age?' the coach was thinking, and that was before the match at the end of the session had even started.

'Wow!' Antonio was soon saying again.

To go with his silky ball skills, Kylian also had electrifying pace. It was a winning combination that the poor Bondy defenders just could not cope with. Every time he got the ball, it was goal-time. ZOOM! Kylian was off, sprinting down the right wing, just like his mum on the handball court. Sometimes, he set up goals for his teammates and sometimes, he scored himself.

1, 2, 3, 4, 5, 6–0!

'Okay, let's switch the teams around a bit. Kylian, put on an orange bib!'

6–1, 6–2, 6–3, 6–4, 6–5, 6–6, 6–7, 6–8!

In the end, Antonio had to stop the game early because he didn't want his players to get too down-hearted. Kylian was simply in a league of his own.

He was better, faster and more consistent than anyone else.

Once practice was over, Antonio went to find Wilfried.

'I don't think Kylian should be playing for the Under-7s,' he explained.

'Why not?' Wilfried replied, looking surprised. 'Did my son play badly today?'

'NO!' the coach replied, laughing at the idea. 'Quite the opposite; he was absolutely incredible! He's the best I've ever seen at that age. The Under-7s league would be a walk in the park for him; he would just get bored. He needs a challenge!'

By the age of eight, Kylian was playing for the Bondy Under-11s, skilling left-backs all game long. He was on a fast track to the top. His killer plan to conquer the football world was going very well indeed.

CHAPTER 4

FOOTBALL, FOOTBALL, FOOTBALL

'No way, Thierry Henry is the best French player ever!' Kylian argued on the walk home with Antonio. 'Did you not see his goal in the 2006 World Cup semi-final against Brazil? And he hit that on the volley too!'

If the Bondy training session finished before Wilfried and Fayza got home from work, Antonio would often go around to look after Kylian for a few hours. The coach didn't do much babysitting, though. Really, it was just two people talking football, football, football.

'Okay, but who set him up with the free kick in the first place? Zinedine Zidane, without doubt the greatest French footballer of all-time!'

'What about the final, though? France were drawing 1–1 with Italy when Zidane got himself sent off. He let the whole team down!'

'That's true but who scored France's goal in that final? Zizou!'

'It was a penalty! Henry could have scored that.'

'Maybe, but Zizou won the World Cup for France back in 1998,' Antonio argued back. 'Those two headers in the final against Brazil – unbelievable! Wait, what year were you born?'

Kylian laughed. 'Nineteen ninety-eight!'

The Bondy coach just rolled his eyes. Sometimes, he forgot that he was talking to someone so young. That was easy to do because Kylian wasn't your average nine-year-old. He didn't just play football; he also spent hours watching it, and knew a *lot* about it. He could talk passionately about his heroes for hours.

When they got back to the apartment, they watched football on TV in the living room, while they had some snacks and drinks. After a short sit-down, however, Kylian was back up on his feet again, moving the furniture.

'Hey, what are you doing?' Antonio asked.

'Just getting the football pitch ready!' he replied.

The Bondy coach shook his head. 'No way, your parents will be furious if we break something! Can't you just wait until tomorrow to play outside?'

It was Kylian's turn to shake his head. 'No, it'll be fine. I've got a soft ball and I play here all the time! But you've got to promise that you won't tell Mum and Dad, okay? Promise?'

Antonio found it very hard to say no to Kylian. He let out a loud sigh: 'Fine, I promise, but only for ten minutes!'

Those 'ten minutes' soon turned into thirty entertaining minutes of 'Henry vs Zidane'. It was a miracle that they didn't break anything. One goal was the sofa and the other was the table. There wasn't much space, so it was all about quick feet and quick thinking. Kylian had both of those, plus home advantage. He knew the living room obstacles to watch out for, and the best angles to shoot from.

Time flew until Antonio suddenly looked at his watch and panicked. 'Okay, final whistle!'

'So, I win?' Kylian asked with a smirk. The score was 10–8 to 'Henry'.

'Yes, this time, but we need to have a rematch soon. Come on quickly, your mum will be home any minute now! You put all the furniture back in the right place, while I clear things up in the kitchen.'

By the time they heard the sound of Fayza's key in the front door, Kylian and Antonio were sitting innocently on the sofa again, as if nothing had happened. They had moved on to their fourth football-based activity of the night – playing FIFA on the PlayStation.

'Hi, Mum!' Kylian called out as the door swung shut.

'Hi darling, how was your day?' she asked, dropping her bag down in the kitchen. When there was no reply, she tried again. 'Kylian, how was your day?'

'Sorry, can't speak right now,' her son replied, tapping the controller furiously. 'Thierry Henry is too busy teaching Zinedine Zidane a lesson!'

CHAPTER 5

CRISTIANO CRAZY!

Thierry Henry was brilliant, but he wasn't Kylian's favourite footballer in the world for long. From 2008 onwards, that was Cristiano Ronaldo. That year, the Portuguese superstar won the Champions League with Manchester United, and Kylian watched every single match on TV.

Like him, Ronaldo was a right winger with lots of speed and skill. He loved to fool defenders with his magical dancing feet. Kylian had never seen anyone do so many stepovers in a proper match. It looked so cool.

'I'm going to do that too!' he decided.

On top of that, Ronaldo was also big and strong.

He battled for every ball and his headers were really powerful. That was an area of the game that Kylian needed to work on, and by the time United took on Chelsea in the final, he was Ronaldo's biggest fan.

'What a goal!' Kylian cheered when his hero scored an excellent header in the first half. He jumped up and down on the living room sofa with his T-shirt up over his head.

'Noooooooo!' Kylian groaned two hours later when Ronaldo's penalty was saved in the shoot-out. By then, the boy's T-shirt was back down on his chest, and he buried his face in it.

But no, John Terry missed for Chelsea and then so did Nicolas Anelka. Ronaldo and Manchester United were the winners!

'Yeeeeeesss!' Kylian screamed. His T-shirt was off and he was whirling it above his head like a cowboy's lasso.

Other than AS Bondy, Kylian didn't really have a favourite football team. Paris Saint-Germain were the biggest club in Paris but they were struggling near the bottom of the French league. Instead, he had lots of favourite football players: Henry, Didier Drogba, Ronaldinho, Lionel Messi, and best of all, Ronaldo.

'Here he comes, "The New Henry"!' Airouche, the Bondy club president, made the mistake of saying one day.

Kylian shook his head firmly. 'No, I don't play like Thierry! I'm a dribbler and a creator, as well as a goalscorer. I'm "The New Ronaldo"!'

'The striker who played for Brazil?'

'No, Cristiano!'

Kylian wanted to know everything about his number one hero. Where did Cristiano grow up? What was he like when he was younger? How did he get so big and strong? Did he have a massive house now, with a cinema room and a swimming pool? What football boots did he wear? What fancy cars did he drive, and how many?

'Once I become a top professional player, I'm going to buy myself TEN beautiful cars!' he told his dad excitedly.

Wilfried rolled his eyes. 'One step at a time, son – you can't get carried away. You'll need to keep improving your skills and you'll need a driving licence too! But football's not about fame and money; it's about success and glory. Has AS Bondy taught you nothing? What's rule number two?'

'Stay humble.'

'That's right!'

Kylian's dad was right; he did still have a long way to go. But Wilfried was wrong about his son's ambition. Kylian's main aim was simple – always to be the best:

The best footballer at AS Bondy...

Then the best footballer in Paris...

Then the best footballer in France...

Then the best footballer in the world, even better than Ronaldo!

The Champions League, the World Cup, the Ballon d'Or – Kylian was going to win them all. The sports cars would just be a nice bonus, a reward for all his record-breaking work.

To keep himself inspired, Kylian decided to decorate his bedroom wall. He pulled out posters from football magazines and cut out images from newspapers too. The action poses changed and so did the kits, but the player in the picture never did.

'It's like a Ronaldo *museum* in here!' Jirés joked. 'You're obsessed, bro!'

Kylian's obsession grew even stronger in 2009 when Ronaldo signed for Real Madrid – for £80 million! It was a new world record transfer fee. After the red of Manchester United and Portugal, Cristiano would now be wearing the famous white shirt worn by the likes of Zizou and the Brazilian Ronaldo.

Kylian had a new favourite football team, and he spent hours watching YouTube videos of his hero's Spanish highlights. Tricks, flicks, free kicks, headers, long-range rockets – there were so many of them! If he kept progressing out on the pitch, Kylian hoped that he too would be worth that kind of money one day. Maybe even more.

CHAPTER 6

CLAIREFONTAINE

By the time Kylian turned nine years old, people in Paris were already talking about 'that amazing boy from Bondy'. At every match he played, there was always a group of scouts watching him.

By the time he turned thirteen, Kylian was ready to take the next big step – joining a top football academy. Playing for AS Bondy was fun, but it was time for a new challenge. After a tough three-day trial, he was one of twenty-two young players from the Paris area selected to attend Clairefontaine.

'You got into Clairefontaine? Wow, that's so cool!' his school friends said enviously.

It was the most famous academy in France and

one of the most famous in the whole world, because that's where French stars Nicolas Anelka, William Gallas and Thierry Henry had all started their careers. For Kylian, joining Clairefontaine felt like a giant leap towards greatness. He was following in Thierry's footsteps!

For the next few years, Kylian would live at the academy from Monday to Friday and then return home to visit his family at the weekends. That sounded good to him, especially when he got to explore the Clairefontaine facilities. It was like a football palace!

They were thirty miles outside Paris in the middle of the French countryside. From his dormitory window, Kylian looked out on beautiful football pitches stretching into the distance for as far as the eye could see. And that was only the start of it. They also had:

An indoor pitch,

A full stadium,

A gym,

And tennis courts too!

'Can I just stay here forever?' he joked with the Clairefontaine coaches.

That was the other amazing thing about the academy. As good as the training had been at AS Bondy with Antonio and his dad, this was ten times better. Kylian was working with France's best youth coaches now, and testing himself against France's best young defenders. Was he good enough to achieve his dream of becoming a professional footballer? That was what he was there to find out.

When Clairefontaine's Director, Jean-Claude Lafargue, watched Kylian in action, he could see the amazing raw talent straight away – the fancy footwork and the incredible pace. However, he knew that talent would need polishing in order to really sparkle at the highest level.

'He's not the best yet,' Lafargue believed, 'but with the right help, he could be!'

The Clairefontaine coaches helped Kylian to improve his weaker foot, so that his dribbling was even more dangerous. If he could take off in either direction, it was so much harder to tackle him.

Stepover to the left, stepover to the right, a little hop, and then GO!

They also helped Kylian to improve his running style so that he was even faster. He still looked a little funny with his long arms swinging, but his teammates weren't laughing when he turned and hit top speed.

'Come on, keep up!' he teased.

Most of all, however, the coaches encouraged Kylian to think about his movement. That was one of the big differences between good players and *great* players. They didn't want Kylian to tire himself out by racing around the pitch. Instead, they wanted him to save his energy for making the *right* runs.

'Look for the gaps!' they shouted.

'What are you going to do when you get the ball?' they asked. 'You've got to be one step ahead of the game!'

'If you can't find space, make space for someone else!' they told him.

Kylian was learning so much, both in the classroom and on the training field, and he was then putting it into practice on the pitch. He scored more and more goals for Clairefontaine and back home at AS Bondy too.

'Watch this!' he told his teammates when he played for them at the weekends. One touch to control the ball and then he was off. *ZOOM – GOAL!*

Kylian was determined to become the best. He was playing more matches than ever but sometimes, that still wasn't enough. He wanted his life to be football, football, football, and even more football!

If he couldn't sleep, Kylian would sneak outside for some extra training. He always kept a ball under his bed just in case. At night, the academy switched their big floodlights off but he used the torch on his mobile phone to guide himself down the stairs and onto the tarmac.

Ahhh! Out in the fresh air, with a ball at his feet, Kylian always felt more relaxed. And with no-one watching him, he could finally practise the latest Ronaldo goal in peace:

'Mbappé has it on the left wing for Real Madrid.

Gerard Piqué and Dani Alves are waiting for him
on the edge of the Barcelona penalty area, but he
fools them both with one simple stepover. Mbappé
dummies to go right, but shifts the ball on to his left
foot instead for the shot. BANG! Straight through the
goalkeeper's legs....

*Gooooooooooooooooooooaaaaaaaaaaaaaaaaalllllllllll
lllllllllllllllll!!!!!!!!!!!!!!!!!!!!*

He had to whisper all this because he would be in
big trouble if the Clairefontaine coaches found him
out of bed.

Kylian loved his time at the Clairefontaine
academy, but it couldn't last forever. At the age of
fifteen, it was time for him to move on to bigger and
better things.

Word had spread about Kylian's talent and all the
biggest clubs in Europe were queuing up to sign him.
He could take his pick, but which one would he
choose?

CHAPTER 7

WHICH CLUB TO CHOOSE?
PART I

One team hoping to sign Kylian was Rennes. They
weren't one of the biggest or richest clubs in France
but they had one major advantage – his older brother
was already playing for their first team.

'You and me in the same amazing attack,' Jirés
tried to persuade him. 'Think how many goals we
could score together!'

It was certainly a tempting idea. Kylian knew
the club really well. When he was seven, he used
to practise his skills on the pitch next door, while
Jirés played for the youth team. Everyone at Rennes
remembered the little boy from Bondy who always
had a football at his feet.

Six years on and people were calling that boy the 'next Henry'. Would he sign for Rennes? Perhaps not, but it was definitely worth a try.

'Would your son like to play for us in a tournament?' one of the coaches asked Wilfried.

'Sure!' said Kylian. He never said no to football.

Wearing the red Rennes shirt, Kylian was head and shoulders above the rest. Once he got the ball, he was simply unstoppable.

'What a player!' the club's coach said enthusiastically. 'We'd love to sign your son for our youth team.'

Wilfried, however, was in no rush to decide. He wanted to make sure that Kylian chose the right club where he would be happy, as well as successful.

'Thank you, we have a lot of offers to consider,' he replied politely.

One of those other offers came from the 2010 Premier League Champions, Chelsea. They sent their scouts all over Europe, looking for the top young talent around. Kylian was soon on their radar and they invited him to come to London for a trial.

'Sure!' he said. He never said no to football.

Kylian loved his time at Chelsea. It was his first experience of being at a big club, and he walked around in a daze.

Wow, the training ground was amazing!

Wow, the Stamford Bridge stadium was really cool!

Wow, there was Didier Drogba, one of his childhood heroes!

Kylian got to meet Drogba, and he got to play some football too. He starred for the Chelsea youth team as they beat Charlton Athletic 8–0.

'You and me in the same amazing attack,' their striker Tammy Abraham tried to persuade him. 'Think how many goals we could score together!'

It was certainly a tempting idea.

'What a player!' the Chelsea coaches said enthusiastically. 'We'd love to sign Kylian for our youth team.'

But still, Wilfried was in no rush. 'Thank you, my son has a lot of offers to consider,' he replied politely.

Kylian left London with happy memories and a

blue Chelsea shirt with his name and Number 10 on the back. That was soon on display on his bedroom wall, next to all the Cristiano posters.

So, what other offers did Kylian receive? Well, every single club in France wanted to sign him, plus Bayern Munich, Manchester City, Manchester United, Liverpool, and even Real Madrid!

The Spanish giants were one of the biggest and richest clubs in the whole world and they had two other major advantages:

1) French legend Zinedine Zidane was their manager

and

2) Cristiano Ronaldo was their star player.

Zidane invited Kylian to come and spend his fourteenth birthday at Real Madrid.

'Sure!' he said. He never said no to football.

It was the best birthday present ever! When Kylian arrived at Real, Ronaldo didn't say to him, 'You and me in the same amazing attack. Think how many goals we could score together!' However, the boy did get his photo taken with his hero.

It was a moment that Kylian would never, ever forget. Wearing a white Real Madrid tracksuit, he stood there smiling next to Cristiano Ronaldo. The superstar even put his arm around his shoulders. No, it wasn't a dream – he had the picture to prove it!

Kylian spent a week at the Real Madrid academy, training with some of the best young players in the world. It was another amazing experience, and it confirmed what he and his family had known all along – that he could compete at the highest level. One day, he was going to be the best.

'What a player!' Zidane said enthusiastically. 'We'd love to sign your son for our youth team.'

Kylian had an offer from Real Madrid, but still, Wilfried was in no rush. 'Thank you, my son has a lot of offers to consider,' he replied politely.

It was going to be the biggest decision of Kylian's young life. Was he really ready to leave France behind? During his time at the Clairefontaine academy, he could go home to Bondy every weekend. If he moved to Madrid, however, Kylian would be much further away from his friends and family. That was a lot for a fourteen-year-old to deal with. But at the same time, could he really say no to Real, Ronaldo's team?

'Remember, it's not "now or never",' Fayza reassured her son. 'There'll be other opportunities. If you don't want to go there yet, no problem. Maybe you'll go there when you're a bit older!'

CHAPTER 8

MOVING TO MONACO

Kylian's mind was made up. For now, he was going to say no to Real Madrid and stay close to his friends and family in France. He was going to sign for a top team with an amazing academy, where he would have the best chance of progressing quickly into the first team.

For all of those reasons and more, Kylian chose Monaco.

The Monaco youth system was the best in the whole of France. The Red and Whites had more scouts in Paris than any other Ligue 1 club, including the local team, PSG! And the Mbappé family had known those scouts for years, ever since Kylian's early days at AS Bondy. They were friendly people, who really seemed to care about his footballing future.

'Your son could be Monaco's next superstar!' they kept telling Wilfried and Fayza.

Kylian's parents had no doubts about that, but was it the right club for their son? Yes! When Kylian visited the Monaco academy centre, 'La Turbie', he was very impressed. The facilities were as big and modern as Chelsea or Real Madrid.

It was also an academy with lots of history. In the past, La Turbie had produced four of France's 1998 World Cup winners – right-back Lilian Thuram, central midfielder Emmanuel Petit, plus strikers David Trezeguet and, you guessed it, Thierry Henry!

'We want to make Kylian the next famous name on that list,' the Monaco academy director told the Mbappé family during their tour. 'This is the best place for him to develop that incredible talent.'

Sold! Kylian loved the sound of that plan. It was the offer that he had been hoping for.

'Welcome to France's greatest football club!' the academy director said, shaking his hand.

At the time Kylian joined their academy, however,

Monaco hadn't won the French league title for thirteen years. In fact, in 2011, they had even been relegated down to Ligue 2. Thankfully, a Russian billionaire called Dmitry Rybolovlev had bought the club and taken them back to the top flight.

'I'm going to lead Monaco to glory again!' Kylian declared confidently.

The club had just spent nearly £100 million on Colombian stars Radamel Falcao and James Rodríguez, but that didn't mean that they didn't care about their young stars. Layvin Kurzawa, Yannick Carrasco, Valère Germain and Anthony Martial had all made the step up from Monaco B to the Monaco first team.

'That'll be me next!' Kylian announced as soon as he arrived.

He couldn't wait to impress his new coaches and teammates. He had a lot to live up to, especially that nickname – 'The New Henry'. Kylian didn't mind the pressure, though. He was sure that he could handle it, even at a higher level.

He wasn't going to let anything stop him from achieving his goals. He always wanted to be the best.

Every time he got the ball in training, he attacked at top speed. ZOOM! He wasn't a show-off, but what was the point in having such silky skills if he wasn't going to use them?

'Excellent, Kylian!'

Leaving his marker trailing behind, he lifted his head up and looked for the pass, just like they had taught him to do at Clairefontaine. If someone was in space, he set them up to score.

'Cheers, Kylian!'

If not, he took the shot himself, and he hardly ever missed.

'Great goal, Kylian!'

Was the Monaco manager, Claudio Ranieri, watching? Kylian hoped so. His masterplan was simple but highly ambitious. He didn't want to sit around and wait patiently. By the end of his three years in the academy, he aimed to be playing for the first team. That seemed realistic to him; it was why he had chosen Monaco in the first place.

If Thierry could do it at seventeen years old, then so could Kylian.

CHAPTER 9

FIRST-TEAM FOOTBALL

After a strong start, however, Kylian's Monaco master-plan was in danger of falling apart. The last of his three academy years had started, and his first-team dream still seemed miles away. Did Monaco's new manager, Leonardo Jardim, even know that he existed? Every day, Kylian grew more and more impatient.

'I don't get it!' he moaned to Jirés. 'What am I doing wrong?'

For years at AS Bondy and Clairefontaine, Kylian had been the coach's favourite and the star player, but not anymore. The Monaco Under-18s manager didn't seem to rate him at all. He was always criticising Kylian for something.

'Track back and help your team!'

'Stop giving the ball away. Pass!'

'Think about what you're doing!'

Kylian was doing his best to improve his game, but his coach's comments were affecting his confidence. At this rate, Monaco might not even offer him a professional contract anyway. He knew that Jirés would understand his frustrations.

'All you can do is try to ignore it and keep working hard,' his older brother told him. 'Everything will work out in the end!'

Those turned out to be very wise words. Kylian's time was coming, and sooner than even he could have predicted.

By 2015, Monaco had stopped spending lots of money on foreign players. That plan wasn't working because the club couldn't compete with PSG in the transfer market. So instead, the club's vice-president Vadim Vasilyev and technical director Luis Campos decided to focus on developing their young French talent. Local players were a lot cheaper and, potentially, a lot better.

One day, while Vasilyev was working on this new idea, he had a visit from a Monaco academy coach, who looked troubled.

'What's wrong?' the vice-president asked.

'We have a talented kid in the youth team, and I think he's going to be a star,' the coach explained.

'Great, what's his name?'

'Kylian Mbappé.'

'Okay, so what's the problem?' Vasilyev asked, looking confused. 'Let's give him a contract!'

Unfortunately, it wasn't that easy because Kylian wasn't very happy at Monaco. He didn't feel wanted by the club and he could no longer see a clear path to the first team.

Plus, he was in high demand once again. He had lots of offers to consider before he signed his first professional contract. PSG were desperate to steal him away from Monaco, and so were Arsenal and RB Leipzig.

Vasilyev went to La Turbie to find out what all the fuss was about. It didn't take him long. Within five minutes, the Monaco vice-president could see that Kylian had phenomenal talent. It wasn't just the speed and the skill; it was also the confidence, the competitive spirit, the fire in the young man's eyes. He seemed to have everything that a young player needed to succeed, and more.

'Wow, why am I only just hearing about this wonderkid?' he thought to himself.

That didn't matter now; what mattered was keeping Kylian happy at Monaco. They couldn't let him leave, especially for free! Vasilyev and Campos went to speak to Wilfried and Fayza about what they could do to help.

'Kylian wants to play first-team football,' his dad said. 'It's as simple as that. I know he's only sixteen, but my son is very ambitious. And very talented!'

Vasilyev and Campos nodded. 'Absolutely, he's one of the most talented young players we've ever seen. Leave it with us; we'll arrange for him to start training with the first team as soon as possible.'

Kylian's first chance came in November 2015. A lot of Monaco's stars were away on international duty, so Jardim needed to call up extra players to take part in the first-team training sessions.

'Get Mbappé,' Vasilyev told him. 'Trust me, you'll be impressed!'

Kylian was so excited when he heard the good news. At last! He didn't feel nervous at all as he walked into the first-team dressing room, and then out onto the first-team training pitch. He believed in himself. This was where he belonged. He couldn't wait to show Jardim what he'd been missing.

ZOOM! Kylian flew past Monaco's experienced defenders in a flash. Now, he had to make sure he finished his run with either a goal or an assist. He had to be more consistent; that was what the Under-18s coach was always telling him. Kylian lifted his head up – did he have a teammate to pass to? No, they couldn't keep up. He would have to go it alone.

The last man backed away, wondering which way Kylian would go…

Stepover to the left, stepover to the right, a little hop, and then GO!

Kylian sprinted into space and fired the ball past the keeper.

Goooooooooooooooooooaaaaaaaaaaaaaaaalllllllllll lllllllllllllll!!!!!!!!!!!!!!!!!!!

Jardim was blown away by Kylian's performance. 'Wow, why am I only just hearing about this wonderkid?' he asked Vasilyev.

The vice-president laughed, 'I asked exactly the same question when I first saw him play!'

'Well, he's not going back to the youth team,' Jardim decided straight away. 'He's a Monaco first-team player now.'

CHAPTER 10

"THE NEW HENRY"

Some young players spend a long time, training with the first team, before they make their senior debut, but not Kylian. He was a hero in a hurry, and who was going to stop him? In December 2015, less than a month after his first training session, he was taking his seat on the Monaco subs' bench!

They were playing at home against AS Caen at the Stade Louis II. The stadium could hold up to 18,000 supporters but it was only ever full for the big games against rivals like PSG. There were only 5,000 in the crowd to watch Kylian's debut against Caen. Well, that was if Jardim brought him on…

'Man, you could make history tonight!' his

teammate, Tiémoué Bakayoko, told him as they watched the first half.

Kylian just smiled and nodded. It was what he had always wanted to do – break records. If he did get onto the pitch, he would become Monaco's youngest-ever first-team player. He was still eighteen days away from his seventeenth birthday. And whose record would he be breaking? Yes, Thierry Henry! That would make it extra special.

Monaco had been struggling to score goals all season. They took the lead against Caen but with five minutes to go, Ronny Rodelin grabbed an equaliser. 1–1!

A draw wouldn't do, though; Monaco needed to win. Jardim turned to his bench. He had already brought on his Portuguese winger, Hélder Costa. Who else did he have?

Paul Nardi – a goalkeeper,

Andrea Raggi – a defender,

Gabriel Boschilia – a midfielder,

Tiémoué – another midfielder,

And Kylian!

Playing a sixteen-year-old was always a risk, but Jardim reasoned that Kylian's speed and skill could be deadly against the tired Caen defence. He was the best option that Monaco had.

'Kylian, get ready,' one of the coaches shouted, passing on the manager's message. 'You're coming on!'

On the touchline, Kylian tucked his red-and-white 33 shirt into his shorts and waited for the fourth official to put the numbers up. Monaco were going all-out attack. Kylian would play on the left wing in place of the left-back, Fábio Coentrão.

'Good luck, kid,' Fábio said as they high-fived. 'Go cause some trouble!'

'I'll try!'

Within seconds, Kylian was on the ball. He controlled Bernardo Silva's pass and then thought about taking on the Caen right-back. Surely he could speed straight past him? No, not quite yet. He decided to play it safely back to Bernardo instead.

'Next time!' Kylian thought to himself.

When Bernardo passed to him again, Kylian faked to cut inside but then – ZOOM! – he dribbled down the wing instead with his dancing feet flying. Eventually, a defender tackled him, but the Monaco fans were impressed already.

'That kid looks brilliant!'

Kylian kept moving and calling for the ball. He wanted it every time. He had the composure to pick out good passes, and the strength to go shoulder to shoulder with his opponents. He was totally fearless. In the end, Kylian couldn't grab the winning goal but that night against Caen, his potential was recognised, and a superstar was born.

'Nothing fazes you, does it?' Tiémoué laughed as he congratulated Kylian at the final whistle. 'You were awesome out there!'

Monaco's wonderkid wasn't getting carried away, though.

'Yes, but we didn't win,' he replied, 'and I didn't score.'

Kylian had been dreaming about his first senior goal since he was four years old. How would it feel? How would he celebrate? And what kind of a goal would it be?

It turned out to be a left-foot shot from near the penalty spot. In the last minute of a home match against ESTAC Troyes, Hélder crossed from the left. There were two players waiting for it – Tiémoué and Kylian. He had sprinted all the way from the halfway line to get there first in a blur of orange boots. He was so determined to score.

Goooooooooooooooooooooaaaaaaaaaaaaaaaaalllllllllllllllll lllllllllll!!!!!!!!!!!!!!!!!!!!

3–1! As his shot hit the back of the net, Kylian turned and threw his arms up in the air. Not only was it his first goal but he had made Monaco history again. Seventeen years and sixty-two days – he was now the club's youngest-ever goalscorer. And whose record had he be broken? You guessed it, Thierry Henry! That made it extra special.

'Fair enough, you finished that well,' Tiémoué laughed as they celebrated, 'but next time, it's my turn!'

Although Kylian was clearly enjoying himself out on the pitch for Monaco, he still hadn't signed his first professional contract. That was a major worry for Vasilyev. Had the club done enough to persuade Kylian to stay? Or would PSG steal him away by offering more money and fame?

No, on 6 March 2016, Kylian sat down to sign a

three-year deal with Monaco. He was where he wanted
to be – playing regular first-team football. He wasn't yet
playing every minute, but he *was* playing lots of minutes.

'I'm very happy and very proud to sign my first
professional contract,' Kylian told the club's website.
'This is the club that has helped me grow. I feel
good here.'

'Right, let's start winning some trophies!' Kylian told
his teammates.

Monaco finished the 2015–16 season in third
place in Ligue 1, a massive thirty-one points behind
the champions, PSG. Still, the good news was that
they qualified for the Champions League. Kylian
was super-excited about that. Even in the thirty-five
minutes of Europa League football he had played against
Tottenham, he had managed to set up a goal for Stephan
El Shaarawy.

Kylian couldn't wait for the challenge of the
Champions League. It was the ultimate test for any
football superstar. Who knew, maybe he would even get
to play against Cristiano Ronaldo's Real Madrid!

Kylian's youth team days at Monaco weren't quite

over yet, though. The Under-19s were through to the final of the Coupe Gambardella against Lens, and they needed their seventeen-year-old wonderkid.

'Sure!' said Kylian. He never said no to football.

Back in Paris at the Stade de France, he was Monaco's matchwinner. He set up the first goal for his strike partner Irvin Cardona with a wicked, no-look pass. 1–0!

The second half, however, was The Kylian Mbappé Show. He used his pace and power to get past the Lens defence and then nutmegged their keeper. 2–0!

Goooooooooooooooooooooaaaaaaaaaaaaaaaaallllllllllllllll llllllllll!!!!!!!!!!!!!!!!!!!

But Kylian had saved his best skills until last. On the edge of the penalty area, he had four defenders surrounding him. Surely, he couldn't escape with the ball! But with a stepover and a burst of speed, he did escape, and he scored too. 3–0!

'Man, you're so good it's not fair!' Irvin joked.

As Monaco lifted the cup, Kylian cheered and bounced up and down with his teammates, but he always kept one hand on the trophy. He didn't want to let it go, even though it would be the first of many.

CHAPTER 11

EUROPEAN CHAMPION

By July 2016, Kylian had become a star for club and country. Because of his parents, he could have chosen to play for Cameroon or Algeria, but instead, he picked France. After all, that was where he was born and where he had lived his whole life. It was the French national anthem that a young Kylian had sung loud and proud with his hand on his heart. Plus, he wanted to be 'The New Henry'.

'If they want me, I want to play for *Les Bleus*,' Kylian decided.

So, did they want him? Kylian played two matches for the Under-17s but after that, his France career stalled. The Under-18s coach, Jean-Claude

Giuntini, refused to select him. Just like his old Monaco youth coach, Giuntini thought Kylian was too inconsistent, too selfish, and not a team player.

Giuntini passed that on to the Under-19s coach, Ludovic Batelli, but luckily, he didn't listen. Yes, Kylian was still only seventeen years old, but he was already lighting up Ligue 1 with Monaco. Plus, Batelli really needed a new superstar because he had just lost his best player, Ousmane Dembélé, to the Under-21s.

'Come on, kid, let's see what you can do,' the coach told Kylian.

France were in the middle of qualification for the Under-19 European Championships. Only eight teams would make it to the big tournament in Germany. To get there, France needed to win their last three matches against Montenegro, Denmark and Serbia. Batelli's team had a strong core – Issa Diop in defence, Lucas Tousart and Ludovic Blas in midfield, Jean-Kévin Augustin in attack – but with Ousmane gone, they lacked flair. That's where Kylian came in...

'Welcome to the squad,' said Lucas, the captain. 'I've heard amazing things about you!'

Not only was Kylian the newest member of the squad, but he was also the youngest. Would he struggle to make friends? No, because he'd been playing with older age groups all his life.

'Are you sure you're only seventeen?' Jean-Kévin joked. 'You act more like you're *seventy-seven*, if you ask me!'

Kylian didn't play football like a seventy-seven-year-old, though. In the match against Montenegro, he was France's danger man. Whether he popped up on the left wing or the right, he was always a threat. He could and should have got a hat-trick of goals and a hat-trick of assists. But instead, it was Ludovic who scored the only goal of the game.

'Come on, where's the end product?' Kylian asked himself angrily. 'You've got to do better than that!'

He did, two days later against Denmark, scoring the first goal in a 4–0 thrashing. Now, France just needed one last win.

Against Serbia, Jean-Kévin dribbled forward and passed to Kylian out on the right wing. 'Finish this!' his brain was telling him. He took one touch to control the ball, then looked up and BANG!

Goooooooooooooooooooooaaaaaaaaaaaaaaaalllllllllll llllllllllllllllllll!!!!!!!!!!!!!!!!!!!!

Kylian and Jean-Kévin high-fived. 'We're off to Germany!' they cheered together.

On the touchline, Batelli punched the air. His decision to pick Kylian was really paying off. Could France now go on and win the Under-19 Euros? Why not? The last time that *Les Bleus* had won it was 2010, when they had Antoine Griezmann and Alexandre Lacazette in attack. Now, they had Kylian and Jean-Kévin.

France were placed in Group B with England, Croatia and the Netherlands. Kylian never worried too much about his opponents. At his best, he knew that he was good enough to beat anyone. Unfortunately, he wasn't at his best in the first game against England. Batelli took him off after sixty minutes as France lost 2–1.

'Don't worry, we all have bad days,' his coach told him. 'In three days, we go again!'

Jean-Kévin scored France's first goal against Croatia, and Kylian scored their second. He controlled Issa's long ball beautifully, dribbled around the keeper and tapped it home. He made it look so easy.

Goooooooooooooooooooaaaaaaaaaaaaaaaaalllllllllll llllllllllllllll!!!!!!!!!!!!!!!!!!!

'That's more like it!' Kylian shouted passionately as he sank to his knees on the grass.

There was no stopping France now, and especially their star strikeforce. They had a friendly rivalry going. Who could score more? Against the Netherlands, Kylian got two, but Jean-Kévin got three!

'I win this time,' the hat-trick hero said as he walked off with the matchball.

In the semi-finals against Portugal, it was Kylian's turn to shine. France were 1–0 down after just two minutes, but they fought back quickly. Dribbling way out on the left wing, Kylian looked like he was going nowhere. But suddenly, ZOOM! – he muscled his way past the Portugal right-back and played a great cross to Ludovic. 1–1!

'Come on!' Kylian cried out as the whole team hugged each other.

In the second half, Clément Michelin crossed from the right, and Kylian poked the ball in.

Goooooooooooooooooooooaaaaaaaaaaaaaaaaaalllllllllllll lllllllllllllll!!!!!!!!!!!!!!!!!!!!

2–1! He celebrated like his hero, with a jump and a spin.

'Nice one, Cristiano!' Ludovic teased.

Kylian's second goal was more like Ronaldo, though. He jumped up high to head the ball past the Portugal keeper. 3–1!

He was France's hero, leading them through to the European Championship final against Italy.

'Okay, you win this time,' Jean-Kévin admitted.

With one game to go, France's two top young attackers were tied on five goals each. Who would claim the Golden Boot?

Against Italy, Jean-Kévin scored his sixth goal in

the sixth minute of the match. 1–0 to France!

What about Kylian? He dribbled into the Italian penalty area, but his shot went wide. 'No!' he shouted, slapping his leg in frustration.

In the end, it was Jean-Kévin who got the Golden Boot and Best Player awards. Never mind that, though, because after a 4–0 win, France were the European Champions! And at the age of seventeen, Kylian had played a massive part in their success. He had another winners' medal to add to his collection.

'Well done!' Kylian's proud parents shouted when they met up with him afterwards.

'Great work!' said the AS Bondy president, Atmane Airouche, who congratulated him. He had come all the way to Germany to cheer his old player on. 'I hope you're having a big party tonight!'

Kylian shrugged. 'Some of the others are going out, but I'm tired. I might just go to bed.'

For Kylian, it was just another goal achieved. The next day, he would move straight on to his next target – winning more trophies at Monaco.

CHAPTER 12

HAT=TRICK HERO

In the space of six short months, Kylian had played his first senior game, scored his first senior goal, signed his first senior contract, and won the Under-19 European Championships with France. All of that, and he was still only seventeen!

So it was no wonder that Kylian was feeling pretty confident as the 2016–17 Ligue 1 season kicked off. He felt ready to fight for more game-time at Monaco. He would show Jardim that he deserved to play more than just the last twenty minutes of matches. He wanted to play every minute of every match! To do that, though, he needed to start the new season with a BANG!

Kylian couldn't wait for the first game against Guingamp. He was starting up front alongside Guido Carrillo, with Tiémoué and Thomas Lemar in midfield. Awesome! However, it soon turned into a nightmare.

First, Monaco went 2–0 down, and then as Kylian tried to turn things around for his team, he suffered a head injury and had to come off.

'What? No, I'm fine to play on!' he argued, but the team doctors stood firm. He couldn't continue in case there was a serious concussion.

For the next two months, Kylian had to wait and watch from the sidelines. Monaco were playing well without him, and they even beat PSG. When would Jardim put him back into the team? Kylian was still as impatient as ever.

Kylian finally returned to the starting line-up against Montpellier. Great, so what could he do to keep his place this time? As he dribbled into the penalty area, he had two defenders in front of him and no teammate to pass to. He faked to cross with his right foot but then switched it to his left. Just as he was about to shoot, one of the defenders fouled him. *Penalty!*

'Well done, mate!' Radamel Falcao said, helping him back to his feet.

Kylian scored Monaco's second goal himself with a clever flick header, and then set up the fourth goal for Valère Germain.

Surely Jardim couldn't drop him after that? But for the next two months, Kylian was in and out of the Monaco team. He would play one great game, and then one average game. That wasn't good enough. He knew that he needed to become more consistent with his goals and assists – and December 2016's League Cup match against Rennes was a good place to start.

Kylian sprinted onto Boschilia's through-ball and curled a shot past the keeper.

Goooooooooooooooooooooooaaaaaaaaaaaaaaaaalllllllllllll llllllllllllllll!!!!!!!!!!!!!!!!!!!!

1–0! 'Come on!' he roared, pumping his fist at the crowd.

Just ten minutes later, Kylian tapped home Nabil Dirar's cross. 2–0!

'Nice one!' he cheered, jumping into Nabil's arms.

Kylian had seventy more minutes to complete his first professional hat-trick. Surely he could do it. The time ticked by quickly, but he didn't give up hope. All he needed was one chance. Finally, in the second half, João Moutinho played the perfect pass and Kylian couldn't miss. 4–0 – he was a hat-trick hero!

'Thanks!' Kylian called out, giving João a high-five and a hug. What a way to celebrate his eighteenth birthday, which was just days away!

Now, Kylian needed to take that red-hot scoring form back into Ligue 1. There was no time to waste. Against Metz, he lined up alongside João, Radamel, Boschilia, Bernardo *and* Fabinho – what an awesome attacking team! Yes, Kylian had a very good feeling about this game...

João chipped a great pass over the top to Radamel, who headed it down to Kylian. With his left foot, he calmly placed his shot in the bottom corner. 1–0!

Gooooooooooooooooooooaaaaaaaaaaaaaaaaalllllllllll llllllllllllllll!!!!!!!!!!!!!!!!!!

'Thanks, partner!' Kylian cheered happily, pointing back at Radamel.

They were Monaco's new star strikeforce, just like Kylian and Jean-Kévin had been for the France Under-19s. Kylian's speed and skill, combined with Radamel's strength and experience – what could defenders do? Uh oh, Metz were in big trouble.

Radamel converted a cross from the right. 2–0!

Kylian raced onto Fabinho's long ball, cut onto his right foot and scored. 3–0!

'Come on!' he cried out, punching the air.

It was time to score another hat trick. Boschilia threaded a great pass through to Kylian. As the goalkeeper rushed out at his feet, he managed to poke it past him. 4–0 – hat-trick hero!

Kylian stood there with his left arm in the air and a huge grin on his face. What a feeling! The Monaco fans waved their red-and-white flags and chanted his name:

Mbappé! Mbappé! Mbappé!

There was even time for Radamel to grab a second goal. 5–0!

'If we keep this up, the title's ours for sure!' Kylian cried out joyfully.

They were playing so well together. With thirteen games to go, Monaco were top of the Ligue 1 table, three points ahead of their rivals, PSG. The fans were full of hope, after seventeen years of disappointment. Kylian and his teammates couldn't let them down.

'Let's take it one game at a time,' Jardim told his players, 'and take our chances!'

Kylian did exactly what his manager asked. Against Nantes, he scored his first goal after four minutes. Then just before half-time, he steered Bernardo's incredible cross past the keeper.

Goooooooooooooooooooooaaaaaaaaaaaaaaaallllllllllll llllllllllllll!!!!!!!!!!!!!!!!!!!!

Kylian roared up at the crowd, pumping both fists. It was another special occasion for him. He had just scored his tenth Ligue 1 goal and he was the youngest player to have achieved that for thirty years. Forget the 'New Henry' nickname – Kylian was on track to become the best player ever!

'Are you surprised by how well Mbappé's

playing?' the journalists asked Jardim. Suddenly, everyone wanted to know everything about France's latest wonderkid.

'No, not at all,' the Monaco manager replied. 'I've worked with him every day since he was seventeen. We know that he's a player of great quality with a spectacular future ahead of him.'

Yes, what a season Kylian was having! His record on the pitch was remarkable – a goal or an assist every sixty minutes. But would he be able to keep that up? Of course he could! He was feeling as confident as ever.

CHAPTER 13

MAGIC VS MANCHESTER CITY

Scoring goals for fun in France was one thing, but what about in Europe? The Champions League was the greatest club competition in the world. That was where a star could become a *super*star. Messi, Cristiano, Neymar Jr… could Kylian be next?

In the group stage, however, he only played twenty-five minutes of Monaco's six matches: thirteen minutes against Bayer Leverkusen and twelve minutes against CSKA Moscow; it just wasn't enough time to shine.

'I'm quick, but I'm not that quick!' Kylian joked with Jirés.

But that was all before he became a hat-trick hero.

By the time the Round of 16 started in February 2017, he was one half of Monaco's star strikeforce – Radamel and Kylian. Would Jardim finally give him his first Champions League start, away at Pep Guardiola's Manchester City?

Yes! There was his name and shirt number on the teamsheet – 'MBAPPÉ 29'. Kylian wanted to run a victory lap around the training pitch but instead, he played it cool. Starting in the Champions League at the age of eighteen? No big deal!

'Thanks boss, I won't let you down,' Kylian said with a serious look on his young face.

Over 53,000 fans packed into Manchester City's Etihad Stadium for the biggest game of the season so far. As the teams walked out of the tunnel and onto the pitch, Kylian's whole body was buzzing. Both sets of supporters were making so much noise! It was even better than he'd imagined in his childhood dreams.

'Attack down the right wing whenever you can,' Radamel told Kylian as they waited to take the kick-off together. 'Fernandinho's a midfielder, not a left-back!'

'Will do!'

It was City who scored first, but Monaco kept fighting. They weren't the best team in defence but they were awesome in attack. Fabinho crossed to the back post and there was Radamel with a brilliant diving header. 1–1!

It was an end-to-end game, full of exciting football. The Manchester City defence couldn't handle Kylian's pace and movement. Radamel flicked the ball on and he sprinted past Yaya Touré and Nicolás Otamendi...

'Keep calm,' Kylian told himself.

He didn't want to waste it by shooting wildly, but unfortunately, that's exactly what he did.

'Hahahaha!' the City fans laughed, as the ball flew high and wide of the goal.

Kylian puffed out his cheeks. What a chance! He had to do better next time. He soon got a second chance. As Fabinho played the pass, Kylian raced into the penalty area, between the City centre-backs. The ball bounced up nicely for him to strike but Kylian didn't rush his finish this time. He slowed down and picked his spot – top corner. 2–1!

Goooooooooooooooooooooaaaaaaaaaaaaaaaaalllllllllll lllllllllllllll!!!!!!!!!!!!!!!!!!!!!

Kylian threw his arms out wide and then slid across the grass on his knees. 'Yesss!' he screamed. He had scored his first Champions League goal, and it was one of his best. Had he broken another record? No, not this time. He was only the second youngest Frenchman to score in the Champions League – Karim Benzema had been three months younger. Never mind!

'What a shot, *Casse-bonbon!*' Benjamin Mendy cheered. That was his new nickname for Kylian. It was the French for 'pain in the neck'.

From then, Monaco's night should have got even better. Radamel missed a penalty and Kylian missed another good chance. But instead, City pulled off an amazing comeback to win the first leg 5–3.

'I know you're disappointed,' Jardim told his players in the dressing room, 'but those away goals could be really important. Now, we have to go and win the second leg at home!'

'Yeah!' they all cheered together. Their team spirit was so strong.

Kylian had never heard such noise at the Stade Louis II. In one stand, the fans formed a wall of red and white.

'Monaco! Monaco! Monaco!' they chanted all night long.

Out on the pitch, the players did them proud. Kylian got his first chance in the sixth minute, but City's keeper made a good save.

'So close!' he groaned with his hands on his head. Still, it was a good sign...

Two minutes later, Bernardo crossed from the left and Kylian stuck out his right boot. Nutmeg! He poked the ball through the keeper's legs and into the net. 5–4!

Goooooooooooooooooooaaaaaaaaaaaaaaaalllllllllllll llllllllllllllll!!!!!!!!!!!!!!!!!!!!!

Kylian hardly gave himself time to celebrate his second Champions League goal. 'Let's go!' he called out, beckoning his teammates to follow him back to the halfway line. They had more work to do.

That early goal gave Monaco lots of confidence. Soon, Benjamin crossed to Fabinho – 5–5! Kylian ran over to high-five the goalscorer.

'We're almost there!' he screamed.

However, when Leroy Sané scored for City, Monaco needed to get another goal, or they were out. They could do it; Kylian never stopped believing. With fifteen minutes to go, Fabinho won a free kick on the right wing. Thomas curled the ball into the box and Tiémoué headed it in. 6–6!   The whole Monaco team chased after their hero.

They would qualify on the 'away goals' rule. An away goal victory was a close as a Champions League tie could be, but Kylian didn't care.'Quarter-finals, here we come!' he yelled to the fans above.

At the final whistle, the players ran towards each other for a big team hug. Against the odds, they had beaten Manchester City!

It was a famous win for the club, and a famous night for Kylian too. He had just scored two goals in two games against one of the best teams in the world.

He was no longer just the talk of France; Kylian was now the talk of the whole football world.

CHAPTER 14

CHAMPIONS OF FRANCE

Kylian's first Champions League adventure didn't end there. He was becoming more and more consistent as the competition went on. In the quarter-finals against Borussia Dortmund in April 2017, he was Monaco's main man again.

Away in Germany, Thomas crossed and Kylian bundled the ball in. 1–0!

Then in the second half, he stole the ball off the Dortmund defence, steadied himself and slammed a shot into the top corner. 3–1!

Goooooooooooooooooooooaaaaaaaaaaaaaaaaalllllllllllll llllllllllllllll!!!!!!!!!!!!!!!!!!!

It was time for Kylian's new celebration pose. He

slid on his knees, folded his arms across his chest, and tried to look as cool as possible. He had his younger brother to thank for the pose. That's what Ethan did whenever he beat Kylian at FIFA.

'You can't keep copying Ronaldo when you score,' Ethan told him. 'You're a superstar now. You need a move of your own!'

Kylian had to use his awesome new celebration pose again in the second leg against Dortmund. It was his fifth goal in four games – he was officially on fire! He scored one more in the semi-final against Juventus but that's where his amazing first Champions League journey came to an end – Monaco lost 4–1 on aggregate.

'I'll be back,' Kylian promised himself, 'and one day, I'm going to lift that trophy!'

He had to move on quickly, though, because Monaco had other prizes to fight for. PSG beat them in the French Cup semi-final and the League Cup final, but their Ligue 1 title dream was still alive.

Game after game, Monaco kept on winning because Kylian kept on scoring. He got the opening goal to beat Bordeaux, and then two more to conquer Caen. His composure was incredible.

'I wish all young players were as mature as you,' Radamel joked in training. 'You're got more sense than Benjamin and Tiémoué put together!'

But every time Monaco won, PSG won too. PSG were still only three points behind in second place. Every weekend, the pressure was on to perform well. One slip-up and the title race could be wide open again.

Monaco's trip to Lyon would be particularly tough. Lyon were fourth in Ligue 1 and they had a talented team featuring Memphis Depay, Mathieu Valbuena, and Kylian's old Under-19 captain, Lucas.

'Come on, six more wins and the title's ours!' Jardim reminded his players before kick-off.

Kylian was determined. They couldn't end their sensational season without a single trophy!

Against Lyon, Radamel scored first but they knew that one goal wouldn't be enough. Monaco needed a second to make things safe. Just before half-time, Bernardo found Kylian in space on the left wing.

Uh oh, Lyon were in big trouble. Kylian licked his

lips and raced forward at speed. He was so dangerous on the dribble. Lyon's centre-back Mouctar Diakhaby backed away and backed away, too scared to attempt a tackle.

Stepover to the left, a little hop, and then GO!

To finish, Kylian lifted the ball over the diving keeper and into the back of the net.

Gooooooooooooooooooooaaaaaaaaaaaaaaaaallllllllllll lllllllllllllllll!!!!!!!!!!!!!!!!!!!!

2–0! Kylian skidded over to the corner flag, with his arms firmly folded. The fans were going wild up above, but not him. He stayed as cool as ever.

'What a hero!' Bernardo cried out when he caught up with his teammate.

Kylian nodded his head as he got back to his feet. Yes, he was a hero – Monaco's hero. And with his help, they were going to win that league title, no matter what.

'Five more wins!' Jardin urged his players on.

The next weekend, Monaco took on Toulouse on the Saturday. Again, Kylian's name was there on the teamsheet and again, it was there on the scoresheet too. There was just no stopping him, or his team. From 1–0 down, they fought back to win 3–1.

'We're nearly there!' Kylian shouted to the supporters at the final whistle.

That Monaco victory put the pressure back on PSG. Could they beat Nice on the Sunday? No, they lost 3–1!

'Two more wins!' Jardim told his players before their match against Lille. The finish line was in sight!

Just before half-time, Kylian found himself one-on-one with the left-back on the edge of the penalty area. Uh oh, Lille were in big trouble. Kylian twisted and turned, one way and then the other, with his fancy feet flashing. First right, then left, then right again. ZOOM! With a burst of speed, Kylian dribbled through and crossed to Bernardo. 2–0!

'Thanks, Kylian!'

In the second half, Thomas chipped a clever pass over the top to Kylian. He could have taken a touch to control it but no, he had a better idea. He could see Radamel waiting in the middle, so he crossed it first time on the volley. 3–0!

'Thanks, Kylian!'

One more win – that was all Monaco needed now. There was a tense atmosphere at the Stade Louis II ahead of their match against Saint-Étienne. Could they claim the title in front of their home crowd? It would be the perfect way to win it.

Monaco! Monaco! Monaco!

Kylian was desperate to be his team's hero yet again. He hit a powerful early strike but the Saint-Étienne goalkeeper made a good save.

'What a chance!' Kylian sighed heavily. Next time, he had to score.

Radamel played the perfect pass and Kylian was off, sprinting straight past the Saint-Étienne defence. Now he just had the keeper to beat. He looked up and picked his spot – bottom corner. He pulled back his right foot and…

…DUMMY!

As the goalkeeper dived, Kylian dribbled around him and passed the ball into the empty net. 1–0!

Gooooooooooooooooooooooaaaaaaaaaaaaaaaalllllllllllll llllllllllllllll!!!!!!!!!!!!!!!!!!!!

'Phew, I thought you were going to miss that!'
Radamel said as they celebrated.

Kylian just laughed. 'Me? Never!'

Would one goal be enough? No, Monaco needed
a second to make things safe but it didn't arrive until
the last minute. Thomas crossed to Valère. 2–0!

By then, Kylian had been substituted, so he stood
there clapping and cheering on the sidelines. Why
wasn't the referee blowing the final whistle yet? He
was ready to run back on for the big title celebrations.

The party had already started in the stadium. The
fans waved their red-and-white flags and sang at the
top of their voices:

Campiones, Campiones, Olé! Olé! Olé!

Finally, the match was over, and so was Monaco's
seventeen-year wait. They were the Champions of
France again!

Campiones, Campiones, Olé! Olé! Olé!

It was a moment that Kylian would never
forget for as long as he lived. He was soon at the
centre of the big team hug on the pitch. Monaco's
superstars moved around the pitch together –

Radamel, Fabinho, Benjamin, Bernardo, Boschilia, Tiémoué, Thomas, Valère, and, of course, Kylian – all applauding the fans.

What an important part he had played in his first full season – 15 goals and 11 assists! And that was only in Ligue 1, where he was the clear winner of the Young Player of the Year award.

In total, Kylian had finished with 26 goals and 14 assists. All that, and he was still only eighteen years old. His stats were way better than Messi or Cristiano at that age. At this rate, Kylian would achieve his dream of becoming the best footballer ever.

Once they had collected their winners' medals and lifted the Ligue 1 trophy, the Monaco players returned to the dressing room to get ready for a big night out.

'Are you coming, mate?' Tiémoué asked.

Kylian shook his head. 'Sorry, I'm tired. I'm going to go home, but have fun!'

For him, the Ligue 1 title was just another goal achieved. The next day, he would move straight on to his next two targets – the Champions League and the World Cup.

CHAPTER 15

FRANCE'S NEW FLAIR PLAYER

'Mbappé for France!'

The Monaco fans had been calling for him ever since the start of the 2016–17 season. 'Yes, he's still young, but look how amazing he is *already*. He could win the World Cup for us in a few years!'

Didier Deschamps, the national team coach, wasn't so sure. What was the rush? At that stage, Kylian was still only seventeen. So, he didn't make the senior France squad for the qualifiers against Belarus in September 2016, or against Bulgaria and the Netherlands in October, or against Sweden in November either.

But by March 2017, Kylian had forced Deschamps to change his mind. How could he say no to

Monaco's young hat-trick hero, especially after his magic against Manchester City? France were crying out for a flair player like that.

'Who knows, maybe we wouldn't have lost the Euro 2016 final if we'd had Mbappé in the team!' his fans argued.

Kylian had watched that final on TV in Germany with the national Under-19s squad. It was France vs Portugal, his nation vs his hero, Cristiano. France were the clear favourites to win. They were playing at home at the Stade de France and their attacking trio – Olivier Giroud, Antoine Griezmann and Dimitri Payet – had looked awesome all tournament.

'Allez la France! Allez la France!' Kylian and his teammates cheered.

In the final, however, France's forwards just could not find a way past the Portugal defence. When Dimitri got injured, Deschamps brought on Kingsley Coman, but he couldn't change the game either. Neither could André-Pierre Gignac or Anthony Martial. In the end, it was Portugal's Eder who scored the winning goal.

'How on earth did we lose that?' France's junior stars asked each other in disbelief. Back home in Paris, their senior stars were asking themselves the exact same question.

'I could have changed that game' – Kylian didn't say it out loud but that's what he was thinking. He had the speed, the skill *and* the confidence. Two weeks later, he helped France to win the Under-19 Euros. If only...

But now, nine months after that Euro 2016 final, Kylian was about to skip straight to the French senior team. Deschamps named his squad for the World Cup qualifier against Luxembourg:

Hugo Lloris, Laurent Koscielny, Paul Pogba, Antoine Griezmann, Olivier Giroud, Dimitri Payet...

There were lots of older, experienced players on the list but there was also a new young star:

...Kylian Mbappé.

'Congratulations!' his proud parents cried down the phone.

'Well done, you deserve it!' his Monaco manager told him.

'You and me, *Casse-bonbon*,' his club teammate Benjamin cheered happily. It was his first call-up too. 'Let's do this!'

What an honour! Being called up to the national team was a dream come true for Kylian, but it wouldn't mean much unless he actually played. If he came on, would he become France's youngest-ever international? He loved breaking records. But no, it turned out Maryan Wisnieski had been thirty-three days younger when he made his debut in 1955!

Still, Kylian was desperate to play against Luxembourg. Hopefully, if France were winning comfortably, he would get his chance.

Djibril Sidibé cut the ball back to Olivier. 1–0!

On the sidelines, Kylian punched the air. They were off to a good start but five minutes later, Luxembourg won a penalty. 1–1!

'Maybe they'll need me to come on and change the game,' Kylian thought, trying to think positively.

But no, Antoine scored from the spot. 2–1!

Then Benjamin crossed to Olivier. 3–1!

Was that game over? Deschamps decided to take

off Dimitri and replace him with… Kylian! He was already warmed up and raring to go.

'Use your speed to attack down the left,' his manager told him.

Sure thing! Wearing the white 'Number 12' shirt, Kylian raced out onto the field. He didn't think about the fact that he was making his senior France debut, or about his talented new teammates. All he thought about was getting on the ball as quickly as possible. How much magic could he create in the last fifteen minutes?

Plenty! Ousmane Dembélé curled a great pass to Kylian as he ran down the wing. Uh oh, Luxembourg were in big trouble. He stayed calm and hit a powerful shot with his left foot, but the goalkeeper managed to tip it over the bar.

So close! Kylian winced. It was nearly the perfect start to his senior international career.

He didn't get another chance to shoot, but he did get the chance to show off his full range of fancy skills and stepovers.

'Hurray!' the France fans cheered. They loved their new flair player.

ZOOM! Kylian sprinted straight past Luxembourg's right-back and crossed the ball into the box. Olivier stretched out his right foot, but he couldn't quite reach it.

So close! Kylian winced again. He had nearly helped Olivier to get his hat-trick.

'Great ball!' the striker shouted, giving him a thumbs-up.

Kylian soon ran out of time but three days later, Deschamps picked him to start in the friendly match against Spain at the Stade de France in Paris.

'Thanks boss, you won't regret it!'

In his hometown, Kylian would get to play sixty, seventy, maybe even ninety minutes of football! He couldn't wait. In the tunnel, he looked as relaxed as ever, but once the match kicked off, he was fully focused on winning and scoring.

A cross came in from the left, and Kylian cleverly flicked it goalwards... but David De Gea made a super save!

So close! For a moment, Kylian stood there with his head in his hands, but then he chased back to get the ball again. He still had plenty of time left.

Kylian certainly didn't look like the new kid on the block. He was linking up really well with Antoine, playing one-twos all over the pitch. Was this the future of France's attack? The fans hoped so.

At half-time, Gerard Piqué even asked to swap shirts with him. What? The Barcelona centre-back had won pretty much everything there was to win in football – the World Cup, the Euros, the Champions League, the Spanish League. But now, Piqué wanted Kylian's shirt!

'Sure,' he replied, sounding as cool as ever.

After sixty-five minutes, Deschamps replaced Kylian with Olivier. At that point, the score was 0–0, but soon, France were 2–0 down.

'That's what happens when you take Mbappé off!' his supporters argued.

Oh well, Kylian's first international goal and assist would have to wait a little longer. That was okay; he would have plenty more chances to impress. At the age of eighteen, he was only just getting started.

CHAPTER 16

WHICH CLUB TO CHOOSE? PART II

After winning the Ligue 1 title for the 2016–17 season, what was next for Monaco? Would they grow stronger, or was it a one-off success? Would they be able to buy even better players, or would they lose their superstars? Unfortunately, it was a story with a sad ending.

Bernardo Silva was the first to go, moving to Manchester City in May 2017.

'I'm going to miss playing with you!' Kylian admitted as they said their goodbyes.

Next, Nabil Dirar went to Fenerbahçe, and Valère Germain went to Marseille, while in July, Tiémoué Bakayoko left to join Chelsea.

'Don't go!' Kylian begged his friend.

Then, to make matters even worse, Benjamin Mendy moved to Manchester City as well.

'No, not you too! Why is everyone abandoning me?' Kylian complained.

At this rate, it would just be him, Radamel Falcao, Thomas Lemar and Fabinho left! Monaco had no chance against the power of PSG, especially when their rivals signed Neymar Jr from Barcelona for £200 million.

'They'll win the league easily now!' Kylian thought to himself.

Was it time for Kylian to move on too? He loved his club but he wanted to win the top trophies. That didn't look very likely to happen at Monaco.

Kylian thought long and hard about what was best for his career. He was one of the top players in the world now, and the big clubs were queuing up to buy him once again. But which one would he choose?

Arsenal? Arsène Wenger had been trying to sign him for years but The Gunners weren't even in the

Champions League anymore. Kylian had his eyes firmly fixed on that prize.

Liverpool? Kylian had an exciting conversation with their manager, Jürgen Klopp, but unfortunately, the club couldn't afford to buy him.

Manchester City? That was a possibility. Money wasn't a problem for them, and Kylian had really impressed Pep Guardiola with his Champions League magic.

'Come join our exciting project,' the City manager tried to persuade Kylian. 'Think about it – you, Sergio Agüero, Leroy Sané and Gabriel Jesus in attack, with Kevin De Bruyne and David Silva in midfield. We would win every trophy there is!'

Working with Guardiola would be an amazing experience, but playing in the Premier League? Kylian wasn't so sure about that – what other options did he have?

Barcelona? With Neymar Jr gone, was there a gap next to Lionel Messi and Luis Suárez? No, they eventually decided to sign his France teammate Ousmane Dembélé instead.

Real Madrid? How cool would it be if Kylian and Cristiano could play together in the same star strikeforce. They would be unstoppable! Real's manager, Zidane, loved that idea and so did the club president, Florentino Pérez. He met with the Monaco chairman, Dmitry Rybolovlev, to agree a deal.

'We want £170 million for Mbappé.'

'We'll offer £130 million, plus an extra £25 million in bonuses.'

Pérez left France, feeling very confident. The deal wasn't quite done yet, but it seemed like only a matter of time before Real got their new Galáctico signing.

Kylian was excited too. He had dreamed of playing for the club ever since his first trip to Madrid for his fourteenth birthday – plus Real had just won the Spanish League *and* the Champions League.

'Don't get your hopes up yet,' his dad told him. 'There's still a lot to work out before you get to wear that famous white shirt!'

Wilfried was also now Kylian's agent and he travelled to Spain to meet with Pérez and the club directors. There was one important issue that he wanted to discuss: Kylian's role in the Real team. After all, he wasn't going to move to Madrid to just sit on the Bernabéu bench.

'So, where will my son fit into the starting line-up?' Wilfried asked.

It was a good question. Real already had their star strikeforce, 'BBC' - Karim Benzema, Gareth Bale and Cristiano. They also had two young talents waiting in the wings: Isco and Marco Asensio. Did they really have space for another wonderkid?

'Don't worry, we'll make room for Kylian,' Pérez promised.

However, by the middle of August, nothing had changed. Real still had all of their attacking stars.

'Sorry, son,' Wilfried said. 'I don't think that's a good move for you right now.'

There was one last option left – Kylian's hometown club, PSG. They were desperate for him to become the third member of their amazing new all-star attack. Forget Barcelona's 'MSN' or Real Madrid's 'BBC'; PSG were aiming for 'MCN': Kylian

Mbappé, Edinson Cavani and Neymar Jr.

'With the three of you, we believe that we can win the Champions League,' PSG's manager, Unai Emery, declared confidently.

That was exactly what Kylian wanted to hear! Not only were PSG offering him regular first-team football, but they were building a top-quality team to take on Barcelona and Real Madrid. He would even get to play with one of his heroes, Neymar Jr! Kylian used to play as PSG on FIFA so that he could use the Brazilian to beat his brother Ethan.

'I'm in!' Kylian told his dad.

There was one big problem, though. Would Monaco really sell Kylian to their biggest Ligue 1 rivals? They didn't want to say yes, but PSG's offer was too good to say no to – the full asking price of £170 million. It wouldn't be paid straight away because PSG had already spent so much money on Neymar Jr, but they would take Kylian on loan for one year and then pay the full amount the next season.

Monaco could see that Kylian's mind was made up. He wanted to return home to Paris and there was no point trying to stop him. On 31 August 2017, the deal was done. Suddenly, his face was seen all over his city.

'Welcome Kylian,' said one poster.

'Paris loves Mbappé,' said another.

Another just showed his number – 29, the same shirt that he had worn at Monaco.

Kylian had already been famous but now that he was a PSG player, he was super-famous. Every time he tried to leave his house, fans surrounded him in seconds, asking for photos and autographs. It was crazy; he couldn't go anywhere anymore!

Oh well, Kylian would just have to get used to all the extra attention. For now, though, he was fully focused on football.

'I really wanted to be part of the club's project,' he had told the media. 'It's one of the most ambitious in Europe.'

It was time for PSG's stars to prove themselves. Kylian, Edinson and Neymar Jr – they were about to take on their greatest challenge together.

CHAPTER 17

OFF THE MARK
FOR FRANCE

Before making his debut for his new club, PSG, however, Kylian had two more games to play for his country. A shock defeat to Sweden meant that France really needed two wins in their World Cup qualifiers against The Netherlands and Luxembourg.

'Let's do this!' Kylian told his old Monaco teammate, Thomas Lemar.

Kylian had only just signed for PSG but luckily, he didn't have far to travel for the first game. The Stade de France was only an hour's bus ride across Paris from the PSG ground at Parc des Princes. He was really looking forward to representing his country again. He was now the second most expensive player in the world, but his international record still stood at four games and zero goals. He had failed to score in twenty minutes against Sweden, or in ninety-five minutes against England.

'I've really got to do something about that,' Kylian told his teammates, with that serious look on his face.

The Netherlands team weren't as strong as they used to be but Didier Deschamps wasn't taking any risks. The France manager stuck with his usual formation – Kingsley Coman and Thomas Lemar on the wings, with Antoine Griezmann and Olivier Giroud up front. That left Kylian waiting impatiently on the bench again.

'Allez les Bleus!' he mumbled, shaking his restless legs. How long would he have to wait?

Antoine played a great one-two with Olivier and then nutmegged the keeper. 1–0!

Kylian slumped a little further down in his seat. If France's strikers kept playing like that, he wouldn't be needed at all! However, sixty minutes went by before Thomas made it 2–0 with a superstrike.

'Bring me on, bring me on!'

Kylian looked over at Deschamps. Was the manager ready to make a change? Yes, he was – and a few minutes later, Kylian finally came on to replace Olivier.

'Hurray, it's Mbappé!' the fans cheered.

Right – Kylian had twenty minutes to score his first goal for France. That seemed like plenty of time but it would soon fly by if he didn't take his chances...

He dribbled through the tired Dutch defence but the keeper saved his shot.

'Hey, look up!' Antoine shouted angrily, standing in lots of space.

'Sorry!'

The next time Kylian ran forward, Kylian did pass the ball to Djibril Sidibé, but he asked for it straight back.

'Now!' he cried out, sprinting into the penalty area.

Djibril's pass was perfect and so was Kylian's finish. This time, the keeper had no chance.

*Goooooooooooooooooooaaaaaaaaaaaaaaaaalllllllllll
lllllllllllll!!!!!!!!!!!!!!!!!!!*

Kylian raced behind the goal with his arms and
mouth wide open. At last, he was off the mark for
France! It was another target achieved before his
nineteenth birthday.

Kylian wasn't his country's youngest scorer ever
but he was their youngest scorer for fifty-four years.
That was a long, long time, and a good reason
to crack out his trademark celebration pose. He
stopped, folded his arms across his chest, and stood
there looking as cool as possible.

'You're allowed to be excited, you know!' Thomas
laughed.

The France players all came over to congratulate
him – Djibril, Paul Pogba, Alexandre Lacazette.
Kylian really felt part of the team now.

'Excellent victory yesterday,' he wrote on
Instagram, next to a picture of his celebration.

At that stage, he was wearing France's Number
20 shirt, but hopefully that wouldn't be the case
for long. Antoine wore Number 7 and Olivier wore

Number 9. Kylian had his eyes on Number 10. That shirt had belonged to Zidane, France's last World Cup hero.

A deadly display in the next match would surely do the trick. Kylian couldn't wait to start in attack with Antoine and Olivier against a nation ranked 136th in the world. Now that he was off the mark, the goals would surely start to flow. Uh oh, Luxembourg were in big trouble...

But no, it turned out to be a really frustrating night for France. They had so many chances, but they couldn't score a single one! Their composure had completely disappeared.

Kylian pulled the ball back to Antoine but he blasted it high over the bar. MISSED!

He played a quick one-two with Antoine but a defender got in the way of his shot. BLOCKED!

Kylian danced through the Luxembourg defence but then fired straight at the goalkeeper. SAVED!

He threw his arms up in frustration. What was going wrong? Were they trying too hard, or not hard enough? Kylian couldn't tell. He showed off his full

range of tricks, flicks and stepovers, but none of it
was working. The score was still 0–0. After sixty
minutes, Deschamps took Kylian off and put Kingsley
on the right wing instead.

'You were unlucky not to score today,' his
manager told him, 'but you've got to learn to take
your chances.'

It was a harsh but very important lesson for
Kylian. Deschamps had so many talented attackers to
choose from: Antoine and Olivier, but also Ousmane,
Kingsley, Alexandre, Dimitri Payet, Nabil Fekir,
Florian Thauvin and Anthony Martial. The pressure
was really on to perform.

Kylian had a £170 million price-tag at club level,
but that didn't mean anything at international level.
In order to achieve his target of playing at the 2018
World Cup, he still had a lot to prove. Deschamps
knew that he could be a gamechanger off the bench,
but was that the role he wanted? No, Kylian wanted
that Number 10 shirt; he wanted to be France's flair
player right from the start.

CHAPTER 18

MCN: THE EARLY DAYS

The PSG fans couldn't wait to see Kylian, and 'MCN', in action, and in September 2017 they got their first opportunity. Uh oh, their first opponents Metz were soon in big trouble.

After thirty minutes, Neymar Jr slipped the ball through for his strike partners to chase. Kylian was desperate to score on his debut, but he let Edinson take the shot instead.

1– 0!

'Thanks!' the Uruguayan said, giving his teammate a big hug.

'No problem!'

'MCN' were going to need to work together

to succeed. They were three superstars but they couldn't be selfish. There was no 'I' in 'team', and especially not in 'great team'.

So, who would score next – Kylian or Neymar Jr? In the second half, Kylian chipped the ball forward to the Brazilian. A defender cleared it but it bounced straight back to Kylian. *BANG!*

Goooooooooooooooooooooaaaaaaaaaaaaaaaaaaalllllllllllll llllllllllllllll!!!!!!!!!!!!!!!!!!!!

2–1! 'Yes!' Kylian screamed out, throwing his arms out wide. One game, one goal – Kylian was already off the mark at PSG.

Who would score next? Neymar Jr, of course! He dribbled through and found the bottom corner. 3–1!

Edinson and Kylian jogged over to congratulate the Brazilian. One goal each for all three of them – what a start for 'MCN'! The 2017–18 season was only just beginning, but the future looked very bright for PSG...

...Just as long as they remembered to work together. The following week they were 1–0 up against Lyon when Kylian won a penalty.

'Hurray!' the supporters cheered at first, but that soon turned to:

'BOOOOOOOOOOOOOOOOOOOOO!'

Edinson had been the team's penalty taker for ages and he was the fans' favourite. But Neymar Jr was trying to steal the spot-kick instead.

'Who does he think he is?' the PSG supporters spat angrily. 'He's only just arrived and he already thinks he owns the place!'

Eventually, Neymar Jr walked away but the Brazilian clearly wasn't happy. To make matters worse, Edinson's penalty then struck the crossbar.

'Come on, we're meant to be a *team!*' Kylian told his strike partners, trying to act as the peacemaker.

'MCN' needed each other. When Neymar Jr missed the next match against Montpellier, 'M' and 'C' couldn't score without him. Kylian had one shot blocked, one shot saved, and one shot cleared off the goal line.

'What's wrong with me today?' he groaned, wiping the sweat off his forehead.

When 'MCN' were reunited a week later against

Bordeaux, they made up for that goalless draw against Montpellier.

Neymar Jr scored a free kick. 1–0!

Edinson poked home the Brazilian's pass. 2–0!

Kylian fluffed his shot but right-back Thomas Meunier scored instead. 3–0!

Edinson let Neymar Jr take the penalty. 4–1!

Julian Draxler volleyed in Kylian's cross. 5–1 at half-time!

The only thing missing was a Kylian goal. He had to get at least one! He vowed he wasn't leaving the pitch until he had added his name to the scoresheet.

Julian returned the favour to Kylian in the second half. Kylian ran on to his pass and picked his spot – far bottom corner. 6–1!

'Finally!' he said to himself with a smile. Kylian dedicated his goal to his injured friend, Benjamin Mendy. He held up two fingers on each hand to make '22', Benjamin's shirt number at Manchester City.

In the dressing room afterwards, manager Unai Emery praised the PSG players. 'See, look what you can achieve when you help each other!'

By the Christmas break, they were nine points clear of Kylian's old club Monaco at the top of the Ligue 1 table. They had won 16 of their 19 games, scoring 58 goals along the way. That included 19 for Edinson, 11 for Neymar Jr and 8 for Kylian.

He wasn't always the star of the show for PSG, but Kylian was the youngest by far and he was just happy to be helping his team out. Along with his eight goals, he also had seven assists. Those were very good numbers and besides, he was looking for club trophies, not individual awards. So far, he was cruising to his second French league title in a row.

He was also learning lots. He had only just turned nineteen and yet he was playing alongside Edinson and Neymar Jr, plus Ángel Di María, Dani Alves, Thiago Silva, Marco Verratti… the list went on and on! With such experienced and talented teammates, Kylian was improving all the time.

'Hey, you're a superstar too, you know!' Neymar Jr kept reminding him.

The Brazilian was six years older than Kylian, but

they got on really well. They were always laughing, joking and posing for Instagram photos together – on airplanes, on the training ground, on the pitch celebrating goals, even at awards ceremonies dressed in smart suits.

'Smile for the followers!'

Kylian was careful not to lose his football focus, though. He was the second most expensive player in the world and the new 'Golden Boy', the best young player in Europe. That was a lot to live up to. Plus, with Ángel playing well, he had to keep fighting for his starting spot. He came off the bench against Dijon with twenty-five minutes to go. Plenty of time to win back his place!

PSG were already winning 5–0, so Kylian could go out onto the Parc des Princes pitch and enjoy himself. With 'MCN' playing together again, the crowd expected more. They got more! Neymar Jr scored the sixth and Kylian scored the seventh.

'Goal time!' he roared, jumping into the Brazilian's arms.

After the match, Kylian posted an Instagram photo

with one arm around Edinson, 'The Matador', and one arm around Neymar Jr, 'Crack x 4'.

Now that they were a happy family, were 'MCN' unstoppable? Not quite. It was easy to forget that Kylian was still so young. It felt like he had been playing football forever! Most of the time, he seemed very mature but occasionally, he did act like the teenager that he was. He was growing up in public and that wasn't always easy.

In the League Cup semi-final against Rennes in January 2018, PSG were winning 3–0 when Kylian took out his frustration on Ismaïla Sarr. It was a silly late tackle and, in a flash, he was surrounded by angry opponents.

'What did you do that for?' they asked, pushing him back.

'Ref, that was reckless. Send him off!' they shouted.

Red card! Kylian walked off slowly, shaking his head and removing his gloves.

'A player did that to me last week and what did he get? Nothing, not even a yellow!' he muttered moodily.

Once he had calmed down, however, Kylian felt guilty and embarrassed. He had let his team down and left them to defend with ten men. What a stupid error! Rennes scored twice, but at least PSG held on for the victory. *Phew!*

'I'm really sorry, that won't happen again,' Kylian promised his manager and teammates. He had definitely learnt his lesson.

'Don't worry, we still won,' Edinson reassured him.

'We all make mistakes,' Neymar Jr comforted him. 'Just try not to make any against Real Madrid in the Champions League, okay?'

CHAPTER 19

KYLIAN VS CRISTIANO

That's right – in the Champions League Round of 16, it was Kylian's 'MCN' vs Cristiano's 'BBC'. At last, he would come face-to-face with his childhood hero on the football pitch. What an exciting encounter! What a fascinating fixture! PSG were cruising to the Ligue 1 title but were they strong enough to challenge Real Madrid, the European Champions?

So far, so good! In the group stage, in the autumn of 2017, PSG had already thrashed Celtic 5–0 and 7–1, and Anderlecht 4–0 and 5–0. That was twenty-one goals scored in only four games!

Kylian's favourite game, however, was the 3–0 win over German giants Bayern Munich. That night,

at the Parc des Princes, 'MCN' had been simply
unstoppable. In the very first minute of the match,
Neymar Jr dribbled all the way across the penalty
area and set up Dani Alves to strike it. 1–0!

Most of the time, Kylian had two Bayern
defenders marking his every move. No problem! He
used his strength and skill to hold the ball up until
Edinson arrived. 2–0!

Again and again, Kylian created great chances
for his strike partners. Edinson and Neymar Jr could
have both had hat-tricks, but in the end, they got one
goal each.

As Kylian went to cross the ball, Bayern's left-
back David Alaba jumped up to make the block. Just
kidding! Kylian rolled the ball across to his other foot
instead.

'Hurray!' cheered the PSG fans of his sublime skill.

Kylian dribbled between Alaba and Niklas Süle,
and this time, he did cross to Neymar Jr. 3–0!

What a night it had been for all three members
of 'MCN'! Although Kylian hadn't scored himself,
he had set up two goals against one of the best

teams in the world. Now, it was time to take on Real Madrid.

The first leg was played away at the Bernabéu. The PSG players were feeling confident as their plane landed in Spain. They were top of Ligue 1, whereas Real Madrid were only third in La Liga. At their best, PSG knew that they could beat anyone, even the European Champions.

'This is it, guys, the match you've been waiting for!' Emery told his team in the dressing room. 'I need you to be fearless out there tonight.'

Kylian looked around at Neymar Jr, Edinson, Marco, Dani Alves, Thiago Silva – yes, they were all fired up and raring to go.

'Let's win this!' the team cheered together.

Kylian liked to think that he was one of the coolest guys around, but even he was shocked by the atmosphere in the stadium. As he walked out onto the pitch, it was like being surrounded by four walls of deafening noise. So that was what 80,000 fans sounded like. Wow!

Looking up, Kylian could see an enormous blue

banner, reading 'VAMOS REAL!' Yes, they were in for their toughest battle yet.

Cristiano took the first shot, but it was PSG who scored the first goal. Out on the right wing, Kylian turned and skipped brilliantly past Marcelo. As he sprinted forward, he had Edinson at the front post and Neymar Jr at the back post. Thanks to Edinson's clever dummy, Kylian's cross ran all the way through to the Brazilian. His shot was blocked but eventually, the ball fell to Adrien Rabiot. 1–0!

'Yes!' Kylian yelled out, pumping his fists. He was playing his part for PSG.

The Bernabéu was stunned into silence, and Cristiano was furious. It wasn't a good idea to anger 'The Beast'. There was no way he was going to let his team lose like that. He scored a penalty just before half-time and then a tap-in with ten minutes to go. The first leg finished Real Madrid 3 PSG 1.

Kylian was hurting as he hugged Cristiano. 'Well played,' was all he could say to his hero.

In fact, 3–1 didn't feel like a fair result at all. PSG had wasted some excellent chances. On the flight home, Kylian couldn't help thinking back to the ones he had missed: the shot that flew straight at the keeper, the cross that he couldn't quite reach.

'Hey, it's not over yet,' Neymar Jr reassured him. 'We can beat them at home!'

The two teams reconvened in Paris the following month, March 2018. As the teams walked out of the tunnel, the Parc des Princes was covered in blue, white and red. They were the colours of PSG, and the colours of France. This time, Kylian looked up at an enormous red banner, reading, 'ENSEMBLE, ON VA LE FAIRE!'

'Together, we will do it.' That's right – teamwork was going to be a key part of PSG's gameplan. They had eleven players out there on the pitch; not just 'MCN'.

Real could have gone 4– or 5–1 up, but with half-time approaching, it was still 3–1. Neymar Jr slipped a great pass through to Kylian. Could he be the PSG hero? The angle was tight but he decided to shoot anyway... saved by the keeper!

'Why didn't you cross it?' Edinson screamed. He

was waiting in the middle for an easy finish.

Kylian put his head in his hands. He had definitely made the wrong decision. 'Sorry!'

It was exactly as Deschamps had told him after France's draw with Luxembourg – Kylian had to learn to take his chances. If he didn't, his team wouldn't win. Early in the second half, Cristiano scored a header: 4–1 to Real!

Kylian's heart sank. That was pretty much game over. Or was it? Edinson did pull one goal back, but that was nowhere near enough. They were out of the Champions League.

PSG 2 Real Madrid 5,

Kylian 0 Cristiano 3.

'Hey, this time we failed,' Thiago Silva comforted Kylian at the final whistle, 'but next time, we'll succeed, okay?'

Kylian nodded but in his head, he was still asking himself, 'Why didn't I square it to Edinson?'

It would take him a few days to get over the disappointment, but thankfully Kylian had other targets to aim for. PSG could still win another French treble.

CHAPTER 20

TROPHY TIME

PSG had won their first trophy of the 2017–18 season way back in July 2017 – the Champions Trophy. Kylian had played that day, but for the losing team, Monaco.

'That one doesn't count!' he decided, and Neymar Jr agreed. He hadn't played in the match at all. In fact, Edinson had been the only member of the 'MCN' trio at PSG at that point.

So, the team really needed to win some new trophies to make Kylian and Neymar Jr happy. PSG were out of the Champions League, but they were top of Ligue 1, through to the semi-finals of the French Cup, and through to the final of the League Cup.

Kylian planned to make the League Cup his PSG Trophy Number One. To lift it, however, he would have to beat his old club, Monaco. In the days before the final, in March 2018, there was lots of friendly banter between Kylian and his old teammates, Radamel, Fabinho and Thomas.

'MCN are coming for you!'

'Ha ha, we're not scared of your three-man team!'

'Yeah, enjoy your runners-up medal, mate!'

When the two teams had previously met in Ligue 1, Kylian played one of his worst games of the season. PSG won but he missed so many chances. This time, he was going to come back to haunt Monaco. With Neymar Jr out injured, the pressure was really on. He had to perform well.

In the eighth minute of the final, Kylian got the ball with his back to goal. He spun quickly and then ZOOM! he was off, dancing his way past Youri Tielemans...

then Jemerson...

then Fabinho...

until finally Kamil Glik fouled him.

'Hey!' Kylian cried out as he got back to his feet.
'That's a penalty. Check the VAR!'

The referee waited for the video assistant's
verdict... *Penalty!* Edinson stepped up and scored.
1–0!

'Yes!' Kylian cheered, throwing both arms up in
the air.

He was only just getting started. Soon, Kylian
was on the ball again just outside his own box,
and he raced forward on the counter-attack. His
pace was so explosive that no-one could catch him.
Just before the halfway line, Kylian looked up and
spotted Ángel in space on the left. His pass was
perfect. 2–0!

In the second half, Kylian dribbled towards goal
again and this time, he poked a pass through to
Edinson. 3–0!

Kylian was desperate to score a goal of his own,
but a hat-trick of assists would definitely do. At the
final whistle, he punched the air and then hugged his
old teammates.

'Man, you tore us apart today!' Fabinho admitted.

Kylian smiled, 'Sorry, your messages just spurred me on!'

Instead of winner's medals, the PSG players got their own small versions of the League Cup.

'Well I know what I'm drinking out of tonight!' Dani Alves joked.

As he celebrated up on the stage, Kylian had his hands full. Not only was he holding a mini League Cup, but he also was also holding the Man of the Match award. As a big basketball fan, Kylian declared himself the 'MVP' on social media – the Most Valuable Player. What a night!

'Hurray!' he cried out, when captain Thiago Silva lifted the big gold trophy.

The next day, Kylian was already asking, 'Right, what's next?' His hunger was never satisfied.

Kylian's PSG Trophy Number Two would be the Ligue 1 title. They were just far too good for the rest of France. They had only lost two league games all season! The PSG squad was so full of stars that they didn't even miss Neymar Jr that much.

Kylian scored one goal with his left foot against

Metz, and then two goals with his right foot against Angers.

'We're nearly there!' he shouted as he celebrated with Edinson and left-back Layvin Kurzawa.

By mid-April, PSG were fourteen points clear at the top of the table. One more win would be enough to claim the title and who were their next opponents? Monaco!

Kylian was desperate to destroy his old club again but unfortunately, Emery picked Edinson, Ángel and Javier Pastore in attack instead. What? No way!

'Sorry, but we've got the French Cup semi-final coming up on Wednesday,' his manager explained to him. 'I need you fighting fit for that.'

Fine! Kylian sat grumpily with the other subs as his teammates scored goal after goal without him. By half-time, they were winning 4–1! He was so bored and frustrated that he started banging his head against the bench seat in front.

'This is torture!' he muttered.

Still, he joined in with the team celebrations at

the final whistle. 'CHAMPION LIGUE 1!' he posted on Instagram with a picture of all the PSG players.

The next day, he was already asking, 'Right, what's next?'

The answer – the French Cup, the final part of PSG's treble! After his rest against Monaco, Kylian was determined to be the star of the show in the semi-final. Uh oh, Caen were in big trouble.

Ángel passed it through to Edinson, who crossed to Kylian. 1–0!

Goooooooooooooooooooooaaaaaaaaaaaaaaaaaalllllllllll llllllllllllllll!!!!!!!!!!!!!!!!!!!

What a great team goal! Kylian leapt into Edinson's arms and punched the air. 'Come on!' he shouted.

Caen equalised just before half-time but PSG's amazing attackers weren't worried. They always believed that they could score another goal.

Ángel backheeled it to Edinson, who crossed to… Kylian again. 2–1!

They celebrated in the same way, except this time, Ángel jumped up on Kylian's back.

'We need a new name for the three of us,' the Argentine suggested. 'DMC?'

Edinson shook his head, and said, 'CMD.'

It was the MVP's turn to disagree. 'No way,' said Kylian, 'it's got to be MCD!'

Thanks to Kylian's twenty-first goal of the season, PSG were through to the French Cup final. Their opponents would be Les Herbiers.

'Who?' a lot of the PSG players and fans asked.

Even Kylian didn't know much about them, and he was the biggest football fan in France! However, he did know everything that he needed to know – PSG were going to beat them!

'Don't underestimate Les Herbiers today,' Emery warned his players before kick-off at the Stade de France. 'They will be so fired up for this!'

But so was Kylian. He really wanted his PSG Trophy Number Three. He was a hat-trick hero, after all.

In the first ten minutes, PSG hit the post twice – first Giovani Lo Celso, and then Kylian.

'How did that not go in?' he groaned, throwing his arms up in frustration.

Ángel headed over the bar and then Giovani clipped the post again! What was going on?

'Be patient,' Edinson told his teammates. 'We'll score soon.'

Giovani was third-time lucky. As he dribbled forward, Kylian made a clever run to create space for him. From the edge of the area, Giovani curled a shot into the bottom corner. 1–0!

'Finally!' Kylian said to himself.

His frustrations, however, continued in the second-half. Kylian thought he had made it 2–0, but no, the goal was disallowed for handball.

'Never, ref!' he protested but it was no use.

Luckily, Edinson soon scored a penalty to secure the win.

'Well done, guys!' Neymar Jr cheered. The Brazilian was still not fit enough to play in the final, but he was back in Paris and proudly wearing the PSG shirt.

'Let me hold it!' Neymar Jr begged as they paraded the French Cup trophy in front of the fans.

Kylian laughed and let his friend hold one of the

handles. Only one, though – he refused to let go of the whole trophy!

That was the end of Kylian's successful first season at PSG – twenty-one goals, fifteen assists and three trophies. A few days later, however, he posed with the four trophies that the club had won, holding up four fingers for the camera.

'You liar, you lost that Champions Trophy final!' Thiago Silva reminded Kylian with a big grin on his face. 'Or were you playing badly on purpose?'

CHAPTER 21

READY FOR RUSSIA

Although the 2017–18 club season was now over, Kylian still had a busy summer ahead of him. Instead of chilling out on a sunny beach somewhere, he would be playing for France at the 2018 World Cup. Hopefully...

Deschamps had so many amazing players to choose from, and only twenty-three of them would go to Russia. Would 'Mbappé' be one of the names that didn't make the list? Kylian would be so disappointed. He had dreamt of playing at a World Cup ever since watching Henry and Zidane back in 2006. It was the tournament of a lifetime and he really didn't want to miss out.

'See you in Russia!' said his Brazilian PSG

teammates Neymar Jr, Thiago Silva and Marquinhos.

'See you in Russia!' said his Argentinian
teammates Ángel and Giovani.

'See you in Russia!' said his Uruguayan teammate
Edinson.

Kylian kept his fingers firmly crossed. He couldn't
be the odd one out. France would need a young flair
player in their squad! But had he done enough to
show Deschamps that he was ready for Russia?

Maybe not in the World Cup qualifiers, but Kylian
was still finding his feet at international level. There
had been lots of exciting signs for the future. He hit
the crossbar in a friendly against Wales, and then set
up goals for Alexandre against Germany and Thomas
against Colombia.

'Now you just need to start scoring goals for
France like you do for PSG,' his younger brother
Ethan said. He was now part of the club's youth
team. 'I know you can do it!'

It was in the next friendly against the World Cup
hosts Russia that Kylian had finally showed exactly
what he was capable of. With Antoine and Olivier

both on the bench, he was France's star striker and he was even wearing the Number 10 shirt. This was his big chance to impress his national team manager.

'Come on, let's show the old guys how it's done!' Kylian told his teammates Paul and Ousmane.

It was Paul who played the perfect pass to him just before half-time. Kylian sprinted between two defenders, cut inside and fired into the bottom corner. 1–0 to France!

Goooooooooooooooooooooaaaaaaaaaaaaaaaaaalllllllllllll llllllllllllllllll!!!!!!!!!!!!!!!!!!!!

'Easy!' he said with a big smile as he high-fived Paul.

In the second half, Kylian scored again and it was one of his favourite goals ever. On the left side of the penalty area, he skilled the Russian defender in two stylish steps:

1) stepover,

2) nutmeg!

It was actually a double nutmeg because his shot then flew through the keeper's legs.

Goooooooooooooooooooooaaaaaaaaaaaaaaaaaalllllllllllll llllllllllllllllll!!!!!!!!!!!!!!!!!!!!

The France fans in St Petersburg went wild for Kylian's classic celebration.

'That's more like it, mate!' Paul teased, slapping his head playfully.

Deschamps was delighted with Kylian's performance. When he was substituted a few minutes later, he got a hug and a big pat on the back from his manager.

'When you play like that, you're unstoppable!'

That's why Kylian was feeling quietly confident as he waited for the France World Cup squad to be announced. With his speed and skill, his manager knew that he could be a real gamechanger.

At last, the list was out. The attackers would be: Antoine, Olivier, Ousmane, Nabil, Florian… and Kylian!

'My first World Cup,' he posted straight away on social media. 'A DREAM!'

When he first joined the national team, Kylian had felt like the new kid at school. Now, however, he couldn't wait to spend the summer with lots of his best friends in football. Benjamin, Thomas, Ousmane, Paul,

Antoine – what a fun group of players France had!

Their World Cup preparations began at Kylian's old youth academy, Clairefontaine. They worked on their tactics and fitness, but most of all they worked on building up the team spirit.

'France feeling,' Benjamin wrote under an Instagram picture of him carrying Kylian around the training pitch on his back. In another photo, Kylian and Paul were wrestling each other on the grass.

Although they all had plenty of laughs together, the France players were deadly serious about winning the 2018 World Cup. Kylian hadn't played in the Euro 2016 final against Portugal but he still felt the pain of that disastrous defeat. It was their job to make the nation proud of their football team again.

Now that he was definitely in the squad, Kylian moved on to his next target – the first XI. After all, there was nothing he hated more than sitting on the boring bench!

Luckily for him, Kylian started all three of France's warm-up matches, and he scored in the last one against the USA. *Phew,* what a relief! So, would that

be Deschamps' first-choice team, with Paul, N'Golo
Kanté and Blaise Matuidi in midfield, and Kylian,
Antoine and Olivier in attack? He really hoped so.

When the squad numbers were announced,
Kylian punched the air. He had got what he wanted –
the Number 10 shirt! Everyone was happy: Paul had
Number 6, Antoine had 7, Olivier had 9, Ousmane
had 11 and Benjamin had 22.

'I've got a great feeling about this!' Kylian told
his teammates as they set off for their World Cup
adventure in Russia.

At their base camp in Moscow, the players had
everything they needed – big luxurious beds, the
best training facilities, and PlayStations for their
competitive FIFA tournaments.

'Get comfortable because we're not going home
until after we win the final!' Deschamps told his
team confidently.

'Yeah!' they all cheered together.

France's first opponents in Group C would be
Australia. They didn't have any famous superstars,
but that didn't mean it would be an easy match; even

Kylian knew that there was no such thing as an easy World Cup match.

He waited impatiently for news of France's starting XI. At last, it arrived and it was… GOOD NEWS! He would be playing up front with Antoine and Ousmane.

'Come on!' Kylian shouted with his fists clenched.

What an honour it was to walk out onto the pitch and represent France at a World Cup. Kylian was desperate to make a big impact, but the Australia keeper saved his only shot of the first half.

'Keep making those runs!' Deschamps encouraged him.

Kylian did, but the pass never arrived. After seventy minutes, Olivier replaced Ousmane and rescued France. He used his strength to set up Paul's winning goal. What a relief! It had been a poor French performance but at least they had the victory they needed.

'We'll have to play way better than that against Peru,' captain Hugo Lloris warned them.

Deschamps' only change for that next game was

moving Olivier into the starting line-up in place of Ousmane. Phew! Kylian would have another chance to prove that he was ready for Russia.

In the middle of the first half against Peru, Paul won the ball in midfield and passed it through to Olivier. His shot bounced off a Peru defender, over the goalkeeper's head and straight to... Kylian! He tapped the ball into the empty net. 1–0!

Goooooooooooooooooooaaaaaaaaaaaaaaaalllllllllll lllllllllllllllll!!!!!!!!!!!!!!!!!!!!

What an amazing moment! At the age of nineteen, Kylian had his first ever World Cup goal! Not only that, but he was now France's youngest *ever* World Cup scorer. Hopefully he would score better goals but there was plenty of time ahead for that. For now, it was time to celebrate. Antoine joined him and copied his classic pose – arms folded, cool looks on their faces.

'*Allez Les Bleus! Allez Les Bleus!*' the fans chanted.

With Kylian off the mark, could France now go on and win the whole World Cup?

CHAPTER 22

AMAZING VS ARGENTINA

Deschamps decided to rest Kylian for the final group match against Denmark. It was a wise move because he wanted his young superstar to be as fresh as possible for France's Round of 16 tie with Argentina.

For the Argentina game, Kylian couldn't wait to face his PSG teammates Ángel and Giovani and, of course, Argentina's Number 10, Lionel Messi. Yes, Cristiano had been Kylian's number one childhood hero but Messi was definitely in his top five. The guy was a total legend!

Times were changing, though. Messi was now thirty-one and Cristiano was thirty-three. Kylian, on the other hand, was only nineteen. People saw him as the future of world football but he wanted to be the present too. He was ready to become a World Cup star, and what better way to show it than by beating Messi's Argentina?

'Come on, if Croatia can thrash them, then so can we!' Paul argued.

Deschamps, however, wasn't getting carried away. 'Any team featuring Messi and Di Maria is dangerous,' the France manager warned his players. 'Of course we can beat them but we need to stay smart.'

The noise was deafening at the Kazan Arena as the two teams walked out for kick-off. France had far fewer fans than Argentina but they sang the national anthem as loudly as they could. Out on the pitch, Kylian did the same, just like he used to as a kid back in Bondy. He was so proud to represent his country at the World Cup.

Kylian started the game brilliantly. As soon as he got the ball, he turned and ZOOM! – he burst through the middle, dribbling all the way to the edge of the penalty area. Eventually, Javier Mascherano had to slide in and bring him down. Uh oh, Argentina were in big trouble.

'Great work, mate!' Antoine clapped. His free kick bounced back off the crossbar. So close!

Never mind, France would get lots more chances because Kylian had done his homework. He knew that pace was Argentina's biggest weakness. At top speed, no-one would be able to catch him.

Five minutes later, Kylian got the ball deep in his own half, and ZOOM! he was off again...

past Éver Banega...

past Nicolás Tagliafico...

past Mascherano too.

What a run! Kylian only had the Argentina centre-back, Marcos Rojo, left to beat. No problem! He kicked the ball ahead of him and chased after it. In a sprint race, there was only going to be one winner. Rojo knew that and so he pulled Kylian to the floor. Penalty!

'Amazing! Are you alright?' Olivier asked as he helped his teammate up.

Kylian nodded glumly. It was so unfair; he was

about to score another World Cup goal! At least France had a penalty, and Antoine didn't miss. 1–0!

Kylian was having his best international match ever. A few minutes later, he sprinted through again and this time, he was fouled just outside the box. Unfortunately, Paul's free kick flew high and wide.

They could have been 3–0 up but instead, Ángel hit a stunning strike to make it 1–1 at half-time. Then, just after the restart, Argentina scored again. 2–1! Oh dear, suddenly France needed Kylian's magic more than ever.

Right-back Benjamin Pavard equalised for France with a glorious goal but they were playing knockout football now. If France didn't score another, the match would go to penalties...

No, Kylian wasn't going to let that happen. This was *his* World Cup. As the ball fell to him in the crowded box, he kept his cool.

First touch to control it,

Second touch to beat Rojo,

Third touch to shoot with his lethal left foot.

Gooooooooooooooooooooaaaaaaaaaaaaaaaaalllllllllll lllllllllllllll!!!!!!!!!!!!!!!!!!!

Kylian skidded across the grass on his knees, with his arms folded across his chest. No big deal! But it was a big deal; it was a *massive* deal. Soon Kylian was at the bottom of a full France squad hug, including all the substitutes.

'Nice one, *Casse-bonbon!*' Benjamin cheered.

Near the halfway line, Messi stared down at his feet, looking devastated.

'Watch out world – there's a new Number 10!' the commentator screamed on TV.

As Kylian jogged back for the restart, he bumped chests with Antoine. His confidence was sky-high and he wanted more. Just in case anyone had missed his first goal, he scored again four minutes later. Olivier fed the ball through and Kylian calmly buried it in the bottom corner. 4–2!

Gooooooooooooooooooooaaaaaaaaaaaaaaaaalllllllllll lllllllllllllll!!!!!!!!!!!!!!!!!!!

The substitutes raced back on to celebrate with France's new World Cup hero. Thanks to Kylian's amazing man-of-the-match performance, they were through to the quarter-finals! Kylian bumped chests with Ousmane, and then thanked Olivier with a hug and a high-five.

'This game will go down in history!' Antoine predicted.

It certainly would because Kylian had become only the second teenager ever to score two goals in a World Cup match. The first? None other than 'The King of Football' himself, Pelé, back in 1958. Wow, what an honour!

With five minutes to go, Deschamps gave Kylian a well-deserved rest. It wasn't a popular decision, however. The supporters wanted Kylian to continue and so did he. He was on a hat-trick, after all! As he trudged off slowly, his name echoed around the stadium.

Mbappé! Mbappé! Mbappé!

Kylian clapped the fans and then accepted a hug from his proud manager.

'Incredible!' was all Deschamps could say.

After the final whistle, Kylian walked around the

pitch with a big smile on his face. He didn't want this amazing moment to ever end. He shook hands with all the Argentina players, including their Number 10.

'Well played,' Kylian said, seeing the despair on Messi's face. Football could be a very cruel game sometimes.

'You too,' the Argentinian replied graciously. 'You were the best player on the pitch today.'

Messi's brilliant football career was far from over but that night, a new world superstar was born.

CHAPTER 23

WORLD CHAMPION

'How are you feeling, Thirty-Seven?' Florian asked as the France players prepared for their World Cup quarter-final against Uruguay.

That was Kylian's new nickname because during that amazing match against Argentina, he had reached a top speed of 37 kilometres per hour. That was as fast as Usain Bolt in the Olympic 100-metre sprint!

'Put it this way; you'll be calling me Forty soon!' Kylian replied confidently.

His teammates were relying on him to be their speedy superstar again in the quarter-finals. It was going to be France's toughest test yet. Uruguay had two deadly duos: Diego Godín and José Giménez at the back, and Luis Suárez and Kylian's PSG teammate Edinson up front.

Uruguay had already knocked out Cristiano's Portugal and now they wanted to do the same to France. Even without the injured Edinson, they were still going to be very dangerous opponents.

'But if we stick to our gameplan, we'll win this,' Deschamps assured his players before kick-off.

That gameplan was simple – stay organised, work hard and work together.

Just like against Argentina, the France fans were outnumbered in the stadium. It sounded like the whole of South America had travelled to Russia for the summer! But Kylian wasn't going to let a loud crowd faze him. He was 100 per cent focused on his target – leading France into the World Cup semi-finals.

Every time Paul or Antoine got the ball in the middle, they tried to set him free on goal. Although Uruguay's defenders were excellent, no-one could keep up with a sprinting Kylian! Olivier tried to set him up too. After fifteen minutes, he headed the ball across goal to Kylian.

'Go on, score!' the France fans urged him. The Argentina match had showed that Kylian was capable of anything.

He had enough time to bring the ball down and shoot, but he didn't realise until it was too late. His header looped up and over the bar.

'Noooo!' Kylian groaned with his head in his hands. What a good chance wasted!

Oh well, there was still plenty of time to make up for his mistake. Kylian ran and ran but this time, he wasn't France's matchwinner. That was okay, though, because winning a World Cup was a team effort. Raphaël Varane and Antoine Griezmann scored the goals to beat Uruguay. 2–0 – job done!

'See you in the semi-finals,' Kylian wrote on Instagram with a big thumbs-up.

But who would their opponents be? On the journey back to base camp, many of the players relaxed by playing cards or watching a movie, but Kylian watched the other big quarter-final between Belgium and Neymar Jr's Brazil on his phone. It was important homework because France would have to beat the winners. The match finished 2–1 to Belgium.

'Bring it on!' Kylian told Antoine on the airplane as he shared the news.

To become the best, France knew that they would have to beat the best. Belgium had an amazing attack too: Romelu Lukaku, Kevin de Bruyne and Kylian's rival Number 10, Eden Hazard. Wow, it was going to be a really great game.

Was Kylian feeling nervous ahead of the biggest game of his life? No, instead he fell fast asleep on the flight to St Petersburg! Benjamin took a sneaky photo and posted it on social media.

'*Casse-bonbon* needs his beauty sleep for the big match!' he joked.

In the World Cup semi-final, France stuck to their gameplan once again. As soon as Paul got the ball in midfield, ZOOM! Kylian was off, sprinting between the Belgium centre-backs. He won that race but sadly he couldn't quite beat their keeper Thibaut Courtois to the pass.

'Nearly!' Kylian thought to himself as he jogged

back into position. He knew that in such a tight semi-final, one goal might be enough to win it.

France had to score first. Antoine played the ball over the top to Kylian who crossed it first-time to Olivier. He stretched out his left leg but his shot trickled wide. They both stood there with their hands on their heads. How many more glorious chances would they get?

Kylian slipped a pass through to Benjamin Pavard but Courtois made a great save.

'Not again!' Kylian muttered to himself. But just when his frustration was growing, France scored, when Antoine curled in a corner-kick and Samuel Umtiti headed it past Courtois. 1– 0!

Kylian grabbed the ball out of the net and booted it high into the air. 'Come on!' he screamed. France were forty minutes away from a place in the World Cup final.

Could they score a second goal to make things safe? Kylian flicked an incredible back-heel pass through to Olivier but his shot was blocked. In the end, it didn't matter because France held on until the final whistle.

Allez Les Bleus! Allez Les Bleus! Allez Les Bleus!

'Yesssss!' Kylian screamed, punching the air. All of the substitutes ran onto the pitch to join in the joyful celebrations. They were now only one step away from lifting the World Cup trophy.

'WHAT A DREAM!' Kylian wrote on Instagram next to photos from the match.

The stage was set for the biggest game of his career – France vs Croatia. At the age of nineteen, Kylian was about to play in his first World Cup final!

On the day of the final, he woke up with a phone full of good luck messages from friends, family, teammates and coaches. He didn't have time to reply to them all but they helped to fire Kylian up for his big day.

'Come on!' the France captain Hugo shouted, clapping his gloves together in the tunnel.

The atmosphere inside Moscow's Luzhniki Stadium was incredible. Supposedly, there were more Croatia fans than France fans, but you couldn't tell from the noise. Both national anthems were sung loudly and proudly. As the Croatia anthem ended, a roar went up around the stadium. It was time for the World Cup final to kick off!

The first half was full of drama but not for Kylian. The Croatia defence was keeping him quiet. Instead, it was Antoine who stole the show with a teasing free kick, and then a well-taken penalty. France 2 Croatia 1.

'We need to calm things down and take control of the game,' Deschamps told his players in the dressing room. 'Stay smart out there!'

That's exactly what France did in the second half. They were more solid in defence and they used Kylian's pace on the counter-attack.

Paul looked up and gave Kylian a great through-ball to chase onto. ZOOM! Kylian got there first, of course, and pulled it back to Antoine. He laid it off for Paul to strike. His first shot was poor but his second was perfect. 3–1!

Game over? No, there was still plenty of time left and Kylian was desperate to grab a goal of his own. When the ball came to him outside the box, he didn't hesitate. BANG! It was in the bottom corner before the keeper could even react.

Goooooooooooooooooooaaaaaaaaaaaaaaaaalllllllllll llllllllllllll!!!!!!!!!!!!!!!!!!

There was just enough time for Kylian's trademark celebration pose before all his teammates jumped on him.

'You legend!'

'What a hit!'

'You did it, 37!'

Allez Les Bleus! Allez Les Bleus! Allez Les Bleus!

What a way for Kylian to end his terrific tournament! Four goals, twenty-one dribbles, one 37 kilometres-per-hour sprint, one Best Young Player award (although Croatia's Luka Modrić would win the Best Player award), and one World Cup winner's medal. All that and Kylian was now only the second teenager ever to score in a World Cup final. He was too old to beat Pelé's record, but the veteran 'King of Football' himself was still very impressed.

'Welcome to the club,' he messaged Kylian on social media, and then sent him a signed Santos shirt.

The next few days were a brilliant blur. But in between all the celebrations, Kylian found time to post not one but TWO photos of him kissing the World Cup trophy.

'HISTORY FOREVER!' he declared.

It took time for the achievement to really sink in – at nineteen years old, Kylian was already a World Champion.

'You might as well retire now!' his dad, Wilfried, joked.

Was there anything left for Kylian to win? Yes, plenty! Luckily, he was totally obsessed with that winning feeling.

After a short holiday in Ibiza, Kylian returned to Paris and moved straight on to his next target – winning the Champions League. Yes, the boy from Bondy had become a superstar, but he was only just getting started.

Monaco
🏆 Ligue 1: 2016–17

Paris Saint-Germain
🏆 Ligue 1: 2017–18
🏆 French Cup: 2017–18
🏆 League Cup: 2017–18

France U19
🏆 UEFA European Under-19 Championship: 2016

France
🏆 FIFA World Cup: 2018

Individual

🏆 UEFA European Under-19 Championship Team of the Tournament: 2016

🏆 UNFP Ligue 1 Young Player of the Year: 2016–17, 2017–18

🏆 UNFP Ligue 1 Team of the Year: 2016–17, 2017–18

🏆 UEFA Champions League Team of the Season: 2016–17

🏆 FIFA FIFPro World XI: 2018

🏆 Golden Boy: 2017

🏆 FIFA World Cup Best Young Player Award: 2018

MBAPPE

7 & 10 · THE FACTS

NAME: KYLIAN MBAPPÉ LOTTIN

DATE OF BIRTH: 20 December 1998

AGE: 21

PLACE OF BIRTH: Bondy

NATIONALITY: French

BEST FRIEND: Benjamin Mendy

CURRENT CLUB: PSG

POSITION: RW

THE STATS

Height (cm):	178
Club appearances:	181
Club goals:	117
Club trophies:	4
International appearances:	34
International goals:	10
International trophies:	2
Ballon d'Ors:	0

★ ★ ★ **HERO RATING: 89** ★ ★ ★

GREATEST MOMENTS

20 FEBRUARY 2016,
MONACO 3–1 TROYES

Just months after his first-team debut and his
seventeenth birthday, Kylian achieved his next target
– his first senior goal! It wasn't his best strike but it still
meant the world to him because he had just become
Monaco's youngest-ever goalscorer! And whose record
had Kylian broken? Yes, that's right, his French hero,
Thierry Henry. A new superstar was born.

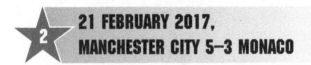

21 FEBRUARY 2017, MANCHESTER CITY 5–3 MONACO

This was the night when Kylian went from being the talk of French football to the talk of world football. It was Manchester City who won this game, but Kylian's speed and skill caused them all kinds of problems. He even had the composure to score a fantastic first European goal.

31 MARCH 2018, PSG 3–0 MONACO

Kylian made the big-money move to PSG in order to win more top trophies. In their first season together, 'MCN' didn't win the Champions League but they did win the French treble. Kylian was the man of the match in this League Cup final against his old club, Monaco. He won an early penalty with one of his deadly dribbles, and then set up goals for Ángel and Edinson. Neymar who?!

30 JUNE 2018, FRANCE 4–3 ARGENTINA

Kylian's match-winning performance against Lionel Messi's Argentina will go down in World Cup history. His phenomenal pace won France an early penalty and in the second half, his two excellent finishes sent them through to the quarter-finals. Kylian became the first teenager since 'The King of Football', Pelé, to score a World Cup double.

15 JULY 2018, FRANCE 4–2 CROATIA

Kylian wasn't at his awesome best against Croatia but he still got what he wanted – a World Cup final goal and a World Cup winner's medal. In the second half, Kylian got the ball just outside the box and buried his shot in the bottom corner. GOAL – what a way to finish off his first fantastic tournament for France!

PLAY LIKE YOUR HEROES

THE KYLIAN MBAPPÉ
SPRINT DRIBBLE

STEP 1: Track back to help your team in defence. It gives you more space for your sprint dribble!

STEP 2: Stay alert at all times. If an opponent plays a bad pass or your team wins the ball, you've got to be ready for the race...

STEP 3: ZOOM! Your first burst of speed is really important. Power your way past as many defenders as possible.

STEP 4: Okay, who's left? If you can beat the last defenders with pure pace, go for it!

STEP 5: If not, you'll need to use your silky skills. Stepover, stepover, stepover, ZOOM!

STEP 6: You're one-on-one with the keeper now, so you've got to stay calm. Pick your spot and shoot.

STEP 7: GOAL! It's celebration time. Run over to the fans, fold your arms across your chest and remember to look as cool as you can.

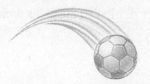

TEST YOUR KNOWLEDGE

1. What sport did Kylian's mum play?

2. Who was Kylian's number-one childhood hero?

3. Which two top European clubs did Kylian visit before joining Monaco?

4. How old was Kylian when he made his Monaco first-team debut?

5. What was the name of Kylian's strike partner as France won the Under-19 Euros?

6. What was the name of Kylian's strike partner as Monaco won the Ligue 1 title?

7. Which country did Kylian make his senior France debut against?

8. Name two clubs (other than PSG!) who tried to sign Kylian in Summer 2018?

9. Kylian won four trophies in his first season at PSG – true or false?

10. How many goals did Kylian score at the 2018 World Cup?

11. Kylian won the FIFA World Cup Best Young Player award, but who won the FIFA Men's Player of the Year award?

Answers below. . . No cheating!

1. *Handball* **2.** *Cristiano Ronaldo* **3.** *Chelsea and Real Madrid* **4.** *16 (16 years and 347 days to be exact!)* **5.** *Jean-Kévin Augustin* **6.** *Radamel Falcao* **7.** *Luxembourg* **8.** *Any of Arsenal, Liverpool, Manchester City and Real Madrid* **9.** *False – he only won three but he posed with all four of PSG's trophies anyway!* **10.** *Four* **11.** *Luka Modrić*

Turn the page for a sneak preview of another brilliant football story by Matt and Tom Oldfield. . .

NEYMAR

CHAPTER 1

OLYMPIC GOLD

'We have to win!' Neymar Jr told his teammates. He
normally liked to laugh and dance before a match but
not this time. He was captain and this was serious.
'Let's get revenge for the 2014 World Cup!'

Neymar Jr was the only member of Brazil's
2016 Olympic squad who had also been there
for that awful night in Belo Horizonte two years
earlier. When Germany thrashed Brazil 7–1 in the
semi-finals on home soil, the whole nation was left
heartbroken. Football was their greatest passion.

But it hurt Neymar Jr more than most because
he was injured for that game and couldn't be the
national hero that they needed. This time, though, as

they faced Germany once again, he was fit and raring to go.

'Germany better watch out!' his strike partner, Gabriel Jesus cheered.

After a long season at Barcelona, Neymar Jr had taken a little while to find his form at the Olympics. As the one of the oldest players in the squad, his teammates depended on him. It was a lot of responsibility and after three matches, Neymar Jr hadn't scored a single goal.

'Don't worry,' the coach Rogério Micale told him. 'That was your warm-up; now we need you at your best in these next big games!'

Neymar Jr scored one against Colombia in the quarter-finals, then two against Honduras in the semi-finals. He had rediscovered his *ginga* rhythm, his Brazilian flair, just in time.

'That means you should score a hat-trick in the final!' his teammate Marquinhos joked.

'No pressure, then!' Neymar Jr replied with a smile on his face.

He led the players out on to the pitch to face

Germany at the Maracanã Stadium in Rio de Janeiro. Nearly 60,000 Brazilians had come to cheer on their country, wearing the famous yellow shirt and waving yellow-and-green flags. They were ready for a party, and the noise and colour were incredible.

Neymar Jr stood with his hand on his heart and sang the national anthem loudly. He was so proud to represent his nation and he was one win away from making everyone very happy. He couldn't wait.

Midway through the first half, Brazil won a free kick just outside the penalty area. It was a perfect opportunity for Neymar Jr. He placed the ball down, stepped back and took a long, deep breath. Then he curled the ball powerfully towards the top corner. It was too quick and high for the goalkeeper to save. The shot hit the underside of the crossbar and bounced down into the back of the net.

Goooooooooooooooaaaaaaaaaaaaaaaaaalllllllllllllllll llllllllllll!!!!!!!!!!!!!!!!!!

Neymar Jr had always dreamed of scoring amazing goals in international finals. Now it was a reality and he would never forget the moment. All of his teammates ran over and jumped on him.

'You did it!' Gabriel shouted.

After the celebrations, Neymar Jr told the others to calm down and focus. 'We haven't won this yet – concentrate!'

Brazil defended well but after sixty minutes, Germany equalised. Neymar Jr had more work to do. He dribbled past one defender and then dropped in a clever Cruyff Turn to wrong-foot a second. It was magical skill and the crowd loved it. He now had the space to shoot. The ball swerved past the goalkeeper's outstretched arm but just wide of the post.

'So close!' Neymar Jr said to himself, putting his hands on his head.

Brazil attacked again and again but they couldn't find a winning goal, even after thirty minutes of extra-time. It was time for penalties.

'I'll take the last one,' Neymar Jr told Micale. He was determined to be the national hero this time.

After eight penalties, it was 4–4. When Brazil's goalkeeper Weverton saved the ninth spot-kick, Neymar Jr had his golden chance. He walked from the halfway line towards the penalty spot with thousands of fans cheering his name.

He picked up the ball, kissed it and put it back down. As he waited for the referee's whistle, he tried to slow his heartbeat down. If he was too excited, he might kick it over the bar. He needed to be his normal, cool self.

As he ran up, he slowed down to try to make the German goalkeeper move early. The keeper dived low to the right and Neymar Jr put his shot high and to the left. As the ball went in, Neymar burst into tears of joy. He had led his country all the way to the Olympic Gold Medal for the first time ever. As he fell to his knees and thanked God, the other Brazil players ran to hug their hero.

'You always said that we could do it!' his teammate Luan shouted. 'Now it's carnival time!'

As Neymar Jr got back on his feet, he listened to the incredible noise of the Maracanã crowd. It was the best thing he had ever heard.

'Imagine what the atmosphere would have been like if we'd made it to the World Cup final and won it in 2014!' Neymar Jr thought to himself, but it was time to forget about the pains of the past and move forward. Thanks to him, his country was back at the top of world football again.

'Thank you!' the coach Micale said to him, giving him the biggest hug of all.

He was still only twenty-four but Neymar Jr had already been Brazil's number one superstar for years. There was so much pressure on him but he refused to let his country down, even after moving to Spain to play for Barcelona.

Neymar Jr had Brazil to thank for everything: the love of his family and friends; the support of his coaches at Portuguesa Santista and Santos; and above all, the amazing skills that he had first developed in street football, beach football and *futsal* matches in São Paulo.